"Do you miss it here? Ever?"

His silence was long. "No, Kayla. I don't have time to miss it."

"If you did have time, would you?"

Again the silence was long. And then, almost reluctantly, he said, "Yeah, I guess I would. Blossom Valley was the place of perfect summer, wasn't it?"

The longing was poignant between them.

"I can't remember the last time I looked at the stars like this," she murmured. But she thought it was probably in those carefree days, those days before everything had changed.

"Me, either."

It was one of those absolutely spontaneous perfect moments. The pure scent of the dew on the grass and the night air and those flowers drooping under their own weight that had made the night so deliciously fragrant.

"Is that Orion above us?" he asked.

"Yes," she said, "the hunter."

"I remembered how you impressed me once by naming all the stars in that constellation."

So she did, naming the stars of the constellation one by one, and then they lay in silence, contemplating the night sky above them.

He didn't answer. He just reached out and slid a hand through her hair, and looked at her with such longing it stole her breath from her lungs.

The air felt ripe with possibilities. Kayla, again, felt seen somehow, in a way no one had seen her for years.

Dear Reader,

I love summer. It has a feeling about it that is light and carefree. I love the summer canvas: afternoons at the beach, swimming in refreshing lake water, going for ice cream, hot nights where you can lie on your back and look at the stars.

This summer threw me some curves, though. My niece, who usually visits me, had to go home just a few days into her stay with a very serious medical condition.

And so the carefree days of summer became threaded through with the weightiness of worry and sadness, and feeling powerless in the face of pain.

I used to think if I did everything right, my life would be a joyous unfolding, unencumbered by suffering. Though it is popular (and reassuring) to believe we can control our world by our attitude alone, my great-grandmother was both wise and realistic. She used to say, "Into every life, some rain must fall."

Over the long days of this summer, I have seen lives where the rain came in torrents. And I have seen people rise to their most inspiring and courageous. Love is my brother-in-law taking weeks off work to be there for his daughter; love is my sister, who sat in the emergency ward, night after endless night, refusing to give up hope, advocating for her child until, finally, finally, an answer came.

Really, this is the story I have been telling for over twenty-five years: of people finding uncommon courage in the midst of strife; finding hope in the hardest of circumstances; finding the resiliency to say a resounding yes to life, even though it can wound. This is love, not on the starlit night, but in the trenches, and I stand in awe of it. I hope this story honors those who showed me love, at its highest and best, over the past few months.

Cara

The Millionaire's Homecoming

Cara Colter

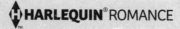
HARLEQUIN®ROMANCE

Recycling programs
for this product may
not exist in your area.

ISBN-13: 978-0-373-74289-9

THE MILLIONAIRE'S HOMECOMING

First North American Publication 2014

Copyright © 2014 by Cara Colter

HARLEQUIN®
www.Harlequin.com

Printed in U.S.A.

Cara Colter lives in British Columbia with her partner, Rob, and eleven horses. She has three grown children and a grandson. She is a recent recipient of an *RT Book Reviews* Career Achievement Award in the Love and Laughter category. Cara loves to hear from readers, and you can contact her or learn more about her at www.facebook.com/CaraColter.

Recent books by Cara Colter

RESCUED BY THE MILLIONAIRE
SNOWFLAKES AND SILVER LININGS*
HOW TO MELT A FROZEN HEART
SECOND CHANCE WITH THE REBEL**
SNOWED IN AT THE RANCH
BATTLE FOR THE SOLDIER'S HEART
THE COP, THE PUPPY AND ME
TO DANCE WITH A PRINCE
RESCUED BY HIS CHRISTMAS ANGEL
WINNING A GROOM IN 10 DATES

The Gingerbread Girls
**Mothers in a Million*

This and other titles by Cara Colter are available in ebook format from www.Harlequin.com.

This story is for my sister, Anna, for my brother-in-law, Dale, and especially for Courtenay.

You are my greatest teachers.

CHAPTER ONE

BLOSSOM VALLEY. IN A fast-paced world, David Blaze thought, a trifle sardonically, his hometown was a place unchanging.

Built on the edges of a large bay that meandered inland from Lake Ontario, it had always been a resort town, a summer escape from the oppressive July humidity and heat for the well-heeled, mostly from Canada's largest city, Toronto.

The drive, two hours—with the top down on David's mint 1957 two-seater pearl-gray ragtop convertible—followed a route that traveled pleasantly through rolling, lush hills dotted with contented cattle, faded red barns, weathered fruit stands and sleepy service stations that still sold ice-cold soda pop in thick, glass bottles.

Upon arrival, Blossom Valley's main street welcomed. The buildings were Victorian, the oldest one, now an antiques store, had a tasteful bronze plaque that said it had been built in 1832.

Each business front sparkled, lovingly restored and preserved, the paned windows polished, the hanging planters and window boxes spilling rainbow hues of petunias in cheerful abundance.

Unfortunately, the main street had been constructed—no doubt by one of David's ancestors—to accommodate horses and buggies and the occasional Model T. It was too narrow at the best of times; now it was clogged with summer traffic.

David, though he had been here only on visits since leaving after high school, found himself uncharmed by the quaintness of the main street, pretty as it was. He still had a local's impatience with the congestion.

Plus, once there had been two carefree boys who raced their bicycles in and out of the summer traffic, laughing at the tourists honking their horns at them....

David shook it off. This was the problem with being stuck in traffic in his hometown. In Toronto, being stuck in traffic was nothing. He had a car and driver at his disposal twenty-four hours a day, and it was a time to catch up on phone calls and sort through emails.

He was accustomed to running Blaze Enterprises, his Toronto-based investment firm, and he had only one speed—flat out. His position did not lend itself, thank God, to ruminating about a past that could not be changed, that was rife with losses.

Then, up ahead of him, as if mocking his attempts to leave the memories of those kids on bicycles behind, he saw a girl on a bike, threading her way through traffic with a local's panache.

The bicycle was an outlandish shade of purple, and the old-fashioned kind, with a downward sloping center bar, high handlebars and a basket. Pedaling away from him, the girl was in a calf-length, white, cotton skirt. The midday sun shone through the thinness of the summer fabric outlining the coltish length of her legs.

She was wearing a tank top, and it was as if she'd chosen it to match the bike. The girl's narrow, bare shoulders had already turned golden from the sun.

She had on a huge straw hat, the crown encircled with a thick, white ribbon that trailed down her back.

He caught a glimpse of a small, beige, wire-haired dog, or maybe a puppy, peeping around her with a faintly worried expression. The dog was sharing the bicycle basket with some green, leafy lettuce and a bouquet of sunflowers.

For a moment, David's impatience waned, and he felt the innocence of the picture—all the things that had been so good about growing up here. The girl herself seemed familiar, something about the slope of her shoulders and the way she held her head.

He could feel himself holding his breath. Then the girl shoulder checked, and he caught a glimpse of her face.

Kayla?

Someone honked at a jaywalker, and David began to breathe again and yanked his attention back to the traffic.

It wasn't Kayla. It was just that his hometown stirred a certain unavoidable melancholy in him. The loss of innocence. The loss of his best friend.

Kayla. The loss of his first love.

Grimly, David snapped on his sound system and inched forward. The street, if he followed it a full six blocks, would end at Blossom Valley's claim to fame, its lakefront, Gala Beach, named not because galas were held there, but after a popular brand of apples that grew in the local orchards.

Gala Beach was a half kilometer stretch of perfect white sand in a protected cove of relatively calm, shallow water. The upper portions, shaded by fifty-year-old cottonwoods, held playground equipment and picnic tables, concessions and rental booths.

It had been a decade since David had been a lifeguard on that beach, and yet his stomach still looped crazily downward when he caught a glimpse of the sun-speckled waters of the bay sparkling at the end of Main Street.

David Blaze hated coming home.

He turned left onto Sugar Maple Lane, and the difference between it and Main Street was jarring. He was transported from the swirling noise and color and energy of Main Street to the deep, shaded silence of Sugar Maple: wide boulevards housed the huge, century-old trees that had given the street its name.

Set well off the road in large, perfectly manicured yards were turn-of-the-century, stately homes—Victorians. Solid columns supported roofs over deeply shadowed verandas. On one he caught a glimpse of white wicker furniture padded with overstuffed, color-splashed cushions that made him think of sugary ice tea in the heat of the afternoon.

And there was the girl on her bike again, up ahead of him, pedaling leisurely, fitting in perfectly with a street that invited life to slow down, to be savored—

He frowned. There *was* something familiar

about her. And then, as he watched, the serenity of the scene suddenly dissolved.

The girl gave a small shriek and leaped from the bike. It crashed down, spilling sunflowers out onto the road. The puppy, all five pounds of it, tumbled out of the basket and darted away, tiny tail between tiny legs.

The girl was doing a mad jig, slapping at herself. It momentarily amused, but then David realized there was an edge of desperation in the wild dance. Her hat flew off, and her hair, loosely held with a band, cascaded out from under it, shiny, as straight as the ribbon around the brim of her hat, the soft light filtering through the trees turning its light brown tones to spun gold.

David felt his stomach loop crazily for the second time in a couple of minutes.

Please, no.

He had slowed his car to a crawl; now he slammed on the brake and shoved the gear stick into Neutral in the middle of the street. He jumped out, not even bothering to shut the door. He raced to the girl, who was slapping at her thighs through the summer-weight cotton of the skirt.

His shadow fell over her and she went very still, straightened and looked up at him.

It wasn't a girl. While he had denied it could be her, his deepest instincts had recognized her.

Despite the snub of the nose and the faint freckles that dusted it, making her look gamine and eternally young, it was not a girl, but a young woman.

A woman with eyes the color of jade that reminded him of a secret grove not far from here, a place the tourists didn't know about, where a waterfall cascaded into a still pond that reflected the green hues of the surrounding ferns that dipped into its waters.

Of course, it wasn't just any woman.

It was Kayla McIntosh.

No, he reminded himself, Kayla *Jaffrey,* the first woman he had ever loved. *And lost.* Of course, she had been more a girl than a woman back then.

He felt the same stir of awareness that he had always felt when he saw her. He tried to convince himself it was just primal: man reacting to attractive woman.

But he knew it was more. It was summer sunshine bringing out freckles on her nose, and her racing him on her bike. *Look, David, no hands.* It was the way the reflection from a bonfire turned her hair to flame, and the smell of woodsmoke, and stars that she could name making brilliant pinpricks of light in the inky black blanket of the sky.

David Blaze hated coming home.

"David?"

For a moment, the panic of being stung was erased from Kayla's mind and replaced with a different kind of panic, her stomach doing that same roller-coaster race downward that it had done the very first time she had ever seen him.

Except for the sensation in her stomach, it felt as if the world had gone completely still around her as she gazed at David Blaze.

She tried to tell herself it was the shock of the sting—knowing that she was highly allergic and could be dead soon—that made the moment seem tantalizingly suspended in time. Her awareness of him was sharp and clear, like a million pinpricks along her arms.

Kayla didn't feel as if she were twenty-seven, a woman who knew life, who had buried her husband and her dreams. No, she felt as if she were fifteen years old all over again, the new girl in town, and the possibility for magic shimmered in the air around her that first time she looked at David.

No, she told herself, firmly. She had left that kind of nonsense well behind her. That pinprick feeling was the beginning of the allergic reaction to the sting!

Still, despite the firm order to herself, Kayla felt as if she drank him in with a kind of dazed wonder. It seemed that everyone she ran into from the old days had changed in some way, and generally for the worse. She'd seen Mike Humes in the hardware store—her new haunt now that she had been thrust into the world of home ownership—and the former Blossom Valley High senior year class president had looked so comically like a monk with a tonsure that she had had to bite her lip to keep from laughing.

Cedric Parson ran Second Time Around— an antiques store that she also haunted, ever on the lookout to furnish her too-large house— and the ex-high school football star looked as if he had an inflated tire tube inserted under his too-tight shirt.

Cedric was divorced now, and had asked her out. But even though she had been a widow two years, she was so aware she was not ready, and that she might never be. There was something in her that was different.

Even the fact that she judged her two high school pals in such a harsh and unforgiving light told Kayla something about herself. Not ready, but also harder than she used to be, more cynical.

Or maybe "unforgiving" said it all.

But trust David Blaze to have gotten better instead of worse. Of course, she knew what he did—the whole town took pride and pleasure in following the success of a favored son.

Even though she'd been back in Blossom Valley less than two weeks, one of the first things Kayla had seen was his picture on the cover of *Lakeside Life*. The magazine was everywhere: in proud stacks at the supermarket, piled by the cash registers of restaurants, in leaning towers of glossy paper at the rental kiosks.

The magazine had recently done a huge spread about his company, and the cover photo had been of David standing in front of the multimillion-dollar Yorkton condo he had developed, in a suit—even her inexperienced eye new it was custom—that added to his look of supreme confidence, power and success.

Though she had contemplated the inevitability of running into him, given where she lived, the photo hadn't really prepared her for the reality of David Blaze in his prime.

How was it that someone who made investments, presumably from behind a desk, still had the unmistakably broad build of a swimmer: wide shoulders, deep chest, narrow waist, sleekly muscled limbs?

David was dressed casually in a solid navy-colored sport shirt and knife-creased khaki shorts, and despite the fact a thousand men in Blossom Valley were dressed almost identically today, David oozed the command and self-assurance—the understated elegance—of wealth and arrival.

His coloring was healthy and outdoorsy. That combined with that mouthwatering physique made Kayla think his appearance seemed more in keeping with the lifeguard he had once been than with the incredibly successful entrepreneur he now was.

His hair, short enough to appear perfectly groomed despite the fact he had just leaped from a convertible with the top down, was the color of dark chocolate, melted. His eyes were one shade lighter than his hair, a deep, soft brown that reminded her of suede.

It had been two years since she had seen him. At her husband, Kevin's, funeral. And that day she had not really noticed what he looked like, only felt his arms fold around her, felt his warmth and his strength, and thought, for the first time, and only time: *everything will be all right*.

But that reaction had been followed swiftly

by anger. Where had he been all those years when Kevin could have used a friend?

And she could have, too.

Why had David withheld what Kevin so desperately needed? David's chilly remoteness after a terrible accident, days after they had all graduated from high school, had surely contributed to a downward spiral in Kevin that nothing could stop.

Not even her love.

The trajectory of all their lives had changed forever, and David Blaze had proven to her he was no kind of friend at all.

David had let them down. He'd become aloof and cool—a furious judgment in his eyes—when Kevin had most needed understanding. Forgiveness. Sympathy.

Not, Kayla reminded herself bitterly, *that any of those things had saved my husband, either, because everyone else—me, his parents—had given those things in abundance.*

And had everything been all right since the funeral? Because of Kevin's insurance she was financially secure, but was everything else all right?

Not really. Kayla had a sense of not knowing who she really was anymore. Wasn't that part of why she had come back here, to Blossom Valley? To find her lost self? To remember

Kevin as the fun-loving guy she had grown up with? And not…

She was weakened by the sting. And by David's sudden presence. She was not going to think disloyal thoughts about her husband! And especially not with David Blaze in the vicinity!

"Where's your kit?" David asked with an authoritative snap in his voice that pulled her out of the painful reverie of their shared history.

"I don't need your help."

"Yes, you do."

She wanted to argue that, but the sense of languid clarity left her and was replaced rapidly by panic. Was her throat closing? Was her breathing becoming rapid? Was she swelling? And turning red? And where was her new dog, Bastigal?

She dragged her eyes from the reassuring strength in David's—that was an illusion, after all—and scanned the nearby shrubs.

"I don't need your help," she bit out again, stubbornly, pushing down her desire to panic and deliberately looking away from the irritation in his lifted eyebrow.

"Bastigal," she called, "come here! My dog. He fell out of the basket. I have to find my dog."

She felt a finger on her chin, strong, insistent, trying to make her look at him. When she resisted, masculine hands bracketed her cheeks, forcing her unwilling gaze to his.

"Kayla." His voice was strong and sure, and very stern as he enunciated every word slowly. "I need to know where your bee-sting kit is. I need to know *now*."

CHAPTER TWO

DAVID BLAZE WAS OBVIOUSLY a man who had become way too accustomed to being listened to.

And Kayla was disgusted with herself for how easily she capitulated to his powerful presence, but the truth was she felt suddenly dizzy, her blood pressure spiraling downward in reaction to the sting. At least she hoped it was the sting!

She divested herself from the vise grip of David's hands on her cheeks, not wanting him to think it was the touch of his strong hands that had made her so light-headed.

He was not there for Kevin, she reminded herself, trying to shore up her strength…and her animosity.

She lowered herself to the curb. "Purse. In the bike basket." It felt like a cowardly surrender.

She watched David, and reluctant admiration pierced her desire for animosity. Even though he was far removed from his lifesaving days, David still moved with the calm and efficiency of a trained first responder.

His take-charge attitude might have been annoying under different circumstances, but right now it inspired unenthusiastic confidence. Feeling like every kind of a traitor, Kayla allowed David's confidence to wash her with calm as she attempted to slow her ragged breathing.

How was it he could feel so familiar to her—the dark glossiness of his hair, the perfect line of his jaw, the suede of his eyes—and feel like a complete stranger at the same time?

David strode over to where she had thrown down her bike, picked through the strewn sunflowers and green-leaf lettuce until he found the purse where it had fallen on the ground. He crouched, unceremoniously dumping all the contents of her bag out on the road. If he heard her protested "Hey!" he ignored it.

In seconds he had the "pen," an emergency dose of epinephrine. He lowered himself beside her on the curb.

"Are you doing this, or am I?" he asked.

He took one look at her face and had his answer. His fingers tickled along the length of her leg as he eased her skirt up, exposing her thigh. She closed her eyes against the shiver of pure awareness that was not caused by reaction to the sting or the feel of the warm summer sunshine on her skin.

She wanted to protest he could have put the pre-loaded needle, concealed within the pen, through the fabric of the skirt, but she didn't say a word.

She excused her lack of protest by telling herself that her throat was no doubt swelling shut. It felt as if her eyes were!

She felt the heat of his hand, warmer than the sun, as he laid it midway up the outside of her naked thigh and pressed her skin taut between his thumb and pointer finger.

"I think I'm going to faint," she whispered, any pretense of courage that she had managed now completely abandoning her.

"You're not going to faint."

It wasn't an observation so much as an order.

She attempted to glower at his arrogance. She knew if she was going to faint! He didn't! But instead of resentment, Kayla was aware, again, of feeling a traitorous clarity she attributed to near death: his shoulder touching hers, the light in the glossy chocolate of his hair as he bent over her, his scent masculine, sharply clean and tantalizing.

Still, some primal fear made her put her hand over the site on her leg where he had pulled the skin taut with his bracketed fingers as the perfect place to inject the epinephrine.

He took her hand and put it firmly out of his way. When she went to put it right back, he held it at bay, his strength making her own seem puny and impotent.

"I'm not ready!" she protested.

"Look at me," he commanded.

She did. She looked into the strength and calm of those deep brown eyes and all of it felt like an intoxicating chemical cocktail so strong it made a life-threatening beesting feel like nothing.

The years dropped away. He was woven into the fabric of her life, the way he cocked his head when he listened, the intensity of his gaze, the ease of his laughter, the solidness of his friendship, the utter reliability of him.

She could feel her breathing slow.

But then with her hand still in the grip of his, her eyes drifted to the full, sensuous curve of his lower lip and she could feel her heart and breath quicken again.

Once, a long time ago, she had tasted those lips, giving in, finally, to that *want* he had always made her feel. Though by then they had both been seventeen, she had been like a child drinking wine and it had been just as heady an experience.

She remembered his taste had felt exotic and compelling; she remembered how he had explored the hollows of her mouth as if he, too, had thought of nothing else for the two years they had known each other.

What a price for that kiss, though! After that exchange, he had gone cool toward her. Frosty. It had changed everything in the worst of ways. They had never been able to get back to the easy camaraderie that predated that meeting of lips.

David had started dating Emily Carson, she, Kevin.

And yet, even knowing the price of it, sitting here on the curb, Kayla had the crazy thought: if she was going to die and had just one wish, would it be to taste David's lips again? She found herself, even though it filled her with self-loathing, leaning toward him as if pulled on an invisible thread.

David leaned toward her.

His eyes held hers as he came closer. She could feel her own eyes shutting, and not just because they were swelling, either. Her lips were parting.

He jammed the pen, hard, against the outer edge of her upper thigh.

The needle popped out of its protective casing and injected the epinephrine under her skin.

"Ouch!" The physical pain snapped her back to reality, and her eyes flew open as Kayla yanked herself back from him, mortified, trying to read in his face if he had seen her moment of weakness, her intention.

It didn't look like he had. David's face was cool, remote.

The indifference of his expression reminded her of the emotional pain she had felt that night after they had shared that kiss. She had thought, on fire with excitement and need, that it was the beginning of something.

Instead, she had become invisible to him.

Just as Kevin had become invisible to him. That was what Kayla needed to remember about David Blaze: he seemed like one thing—a man you could count on with your life, in fact—and yet when there was any kind of *emotional* need involved, he could not be relied on at all.

The moment of feeling intoxicated by David was gone like a soap bubble that had floated upward, iridescent and ethereal, and then *pop*—over.

"That hurt," she said. It was the memories of all the ways he had disappointed her as much as the injection, not that he needed to know.

"Sorry," he said with utter insincerity. He hadn't cared about her pain or Kevin's back then, and he didn't care now. He got up, moved to his car with efficiency of motion. It seemed as if he were unhurried and yet he was back at her side almost before she could blink.

He settled back on the curb, and Kayla ordered herself not to take any more comfort from the strength in the shoulder that touched hers. She saw David had retrieved a small first-aid kit from the glove box of his car, and he unzipped it and rummaged through, coming up with a pair of tweezers.

"I'm just going to see if I can find the stinger."

"You are not!" she said, yanking her skirt down over her naked thigh and pressing the fabric tight to her legs.

"Don't be ridiculous. The stinger could still be pumping poison into you."

She hesitated and he, sensing her hesitation, pressed. "I already saw the sting site. And your panties. They're pink."

To match the blush she could feel moving up her cheeks. Kayla sputtered ineffectually as he easily overpowered her attempts to hold her skirt down.

"There it is. Quit jumping around like that."

"Give me those tweezers!" She made a grab for them.

"Stay calm, Kayla," he ordered, amused.

"It's like being bitten by a snake. The more excited you get, the worse it is."

"I don't want you messing around under my skirt and talking about excitement," she said grimly.

But for the first time, his stern mask fell. He gave a small snort of laughter, and that damned grin made him more astoundingly attractive than ever! "Just be grateful you didn't get stung somewhere else."

"Grateful," she muttered. "I'll be sure and add it to my list."

"Got it!" he said with satisfaction, inspecting the tweezers and then holding them up for her to see. Sure enough, a hair of a stinger was trapped in them.

The amusement that had briefly made him so attractive had completely evaporated.

"Get in the car."

That's what she had to remember. The very qualities that made David a superb rescuer—detachment, a certain hard-nosed ability to do what needed to be done—also made him impossible to get close to.

What had she been thinking, leaning toward him, thinking of his kiss?

She was in shock, that was all. Riding her bike with her dog and sunflowers on a perfect summer day when out of nowhere, a bee. And him.

She, of all people, should know that. When you least expected it, life wreaked havoc. It was a mistake to surrender control, and the circumstances were no longer life-threatening, so she simply wasn't giving in.

"My dog," she reminded him. "And my bike. My purse. My stuff is all over the road. The phone is new. I need to—"

"You need to get in the car," David said, enunciating every word with a certain grim patience.

"No," she said, enunciating every word as carefully as he did, "I need to find my dog. And get my bike off the street. And retrieve my phone. It is a very expensive phone."

He frowned, a man who moved in a world where his power was absolute. He was unaccustomed to anyone saying no to him, and she felt a certain childish satisfaction at the surprised, annoyed look on his face.

Slowly, as if he was speaking to a child, and not a very bright one at that, David said, "I'm taking you to the emergency clinic. I'm doing it now."

"Thank you. You've given me the shot. I undoubtedly owe you my life, but—"

"I'll take care of the dog and the bike and

the purse and the phone after I've made sure you are all right."

"I *am* all right!"

That was, in fact, a lie. Kayla felt quite woozy.

And she got the impression he was not the least bit fooled as he looked at her carefully.

"Get in the car," he said again.

He was quite maddening in his authoritative approach to her. Her gaze went to her personal belongings scattered all over the road. "The EpiPen bought me time," she said, tilting her chin stubbornly at him.

His sigh seemed long-suffering, though their encounter had lasted only minutes. "Kayla, you need to listen to me. I'll take care of your stuff after I've taken care of you."

She scanned his face, the stern, no-nonsense cast of his features, and felt a somewhat aggravating sense of relief swell in her. Why would it feel quite good to surrender control to him? To let someone else be in charge? To let someone else take care of her?

David was just *that* guy, and he always had been. The one who did everything right. The one who knew what to do. The one who could be counted on to look after things. The one you would choose to have with you in an emergency: when the hurricane arrived, or the boat capsized or the house caught fire.

Except he hadn't done the right thing by Kevin, the time it had really counted.

"My dog is on the loose somewhere. He could be picked up by a stranger or run over by a car. My bike could be stolen. The new phone could be crushed by a passing vehicle!"

Irrationally, she trusted David, in some areas, at least. If he said he'd take care of it, he simply would. His strength of purpose had always been nothing less than amazing.

And intolerant of those less strong.

Like Kevin, who had never taken care of anything.

The thought, breathtaking in its disloyalty, came out of nowhere, blasted her and made her feel guilty. And, oddly, angry at David all over again.

Okay, so Kevin had not been overly responsible. He'd had many great qualities!

Hadn't he? The whisper of disloyalty, again, made her feel angry with David as if his presence was nursing these forbidden thoughts to the forefront.

"I need to find my dog," she said, folding her arms over her chest. She was not going to have these thoughts, or surrender control to David Blaze—who was overly responsible—without so much as a whimper.

Had she learned nothing from life? No, she had learned to rely on herself!

"I'm okay now," she said, and it felt like an act of supreme bravery, in light of his darkening features. "David, I appreciate you playing knight in shining armor to my damsel in distress."

The look on his face darkened so she rushed on, shooting a look at his car, "I appreciate your riding in on your shining gray steed, but really, I'll take it from here. I don't need any more help from you."

CHAPTER THREE

DAVID CONTEMPLATED KAYLA, and it was hard not to shirk from the impatience that yanked at the muscle in his jaw and darkened his eyes to a shade of brown so dark it bordered on being black.

He looked totally formidable, and not a single remnant of the carefree boy of Kayla's adolescence appeared to remain in him.

When had he become this? A man so totally certain of his own power, a man not to be messed with?

"I'm not playing a game here," he said quietly. "I am not playing knight to your princess. Not even close. Life is not a fairy tale."

"I'm the last person who needs to be reminded of that," she said, and he flinched, ever so faintly, but still she had to hide a shiver at his intensity, and her face felt suddenly hot.

She was not blushing at the thought of sharing a fairy tale with him! It occurred to Kayla that, despite the shot, her face might be swelling. In fact, with each passing second she probably was looking more like poor Quasimodo, with his misshapen face, than a princess.

"You are highly allergic to beestings," he said, his patience worn thin, like a scientist trying to explain a highly complicated formula to a fool. "Anaphylaxis is a life-threatening emergency."

She touched her forehead. She could feel the puffiness in it.

"We have stopped the emergency for now," he went on. "A secondary reaction is not uncommon. You need to be under medical observation."

"But my dog," she said, weakly. She knew he had already won, even before he snapped *"Enough,"* with a quiet authority that made her stomach dip.

"Kayla, either get to the car under your own power, or I'll throw you over my shoulder and put you there with mine."

She scanned his face, and could feel the heat in her own intensify. There was no doubt at all in her mind that he meant it.

Or that her forehead felt like it was swelling like a balloon filling with helium.

"Humph." She stuck her chin out, but it was

a token protest. As annoying as it was, he was absolutely right.

By the time his hand went to her elbow and he used his easy strength to leverage her up, Kayla had no resistance in her at all.

Annoyed with herself, she shook off his hand, marched to his car, opened the passenger-side door and slid in. The deep leather seat had been warmed by the sun, and the rich scent of the luxurious car enveloped her.

It was possibly the nicest car Kayla had ever been in. Her car, now, was a presentable, fairly new economy model that Kevin's insurance had allowed.

She didn't even want to think about the cars before that—a string of dilapidated jalopies that always seemed to need repairs she and Kevin could never afford.

That made her even more determined not to give David the satisfaction of thinking his beautiful car made any kind of impression on her.

Apparently not any more interested in small talk than she was, David got in the driver's side. He checked over his shoulder, pulled out into the empty street, did a tight U-turn and headed back toward downtown, though he had a local's savvy for navigating a path around the congested main street toward the beach.

Kayla settled her head against the back of her seat and felt a subtle, contented lethargy. The aftermath of the sting, or the drug hitting her system, or surrendering control or some lethal combination of all of those things.

She had always had a secret desire to ride in a convertible, and even though the circumstances were not quite as she had envisioned, she did not know if the opportunity would ever arise again.

She tugged at the elastic that most of her hair had fallen out of anyway, and freed her hair to the wind. If the circumstances had been different, she had a feeling this experience would be intoxicatingly pleasurable.

David glanced at her, and his eyes seemed to hold on her hair before he looked at her face and a reluctant smile tugged at the beautiful corner of his mouth.

Kayla flipped down the sun visor on her side, and it explained the smile. Despite the adrenaline shot, her brow bone had disappeared into puffiness that was forming a shelf over her eyes. She could have hidden under her hat if it wasn't lying back there on the road waiting to get run over with the rest of her things!

Including her dog. Surely, he could have taken a moment to find the dog.

But no, she came first.

A long time since she had come first. Not that it was personal. It was an emergency responder prioritizing.

She cast David a glance. Thankfully, he had turned his attention back to the road. He was an excellent driver, alert and relaxed at the same time, fast but controlled. His face had a stubborn set to it. He had, in that infernally aggravating way of his, put his priorities in order, and a dog was not among them!

"Can I borrow your cell phone?" Her voice came out faintly slurred over a thick tongue, and much as the admission hurt, Kayla knew he had made the right decision.

He fished the phone out of his pocket and tossed it to her casually.

Who to call about the dog? She barely knew anyone here anymore. The neighbors across the street had their name on their mailbox. And children home for the summer.

She navigated his phone to a local directory, looked up her neighbor's number and asked whether her kids could look for the dog. She offered a reward, and then as an afterthought, payment if they would go collect her bike and belongings.

"I said I'd look after it," he said when she clicked off.

She gave him a frosty look that she hoped,

despite the swollen brow, let him know she would look after her own life, thank you very much.

Despite her discomfort, Kayla could not help but notice the details of the gorgeous vehicle. Sleek and posh, the subtle statement of a man who had parlayed his substantial talent for being able to discern the right thing into a sizable fortune and an amazing success story.

Not like Kevin.

Again, the thought came from nowhere, as if somehow David's close proximity was coaxing to the surface feelings she did not want to acknowledge about her late husband.

Guilt washed over her. And then she just felt angry. She had tried so, so hard to put Kevin back together again, and not a word from David.

The ride with him was mercifully short given that his scent—masculine and clean—was mingling with the scent of sun on leather, and tickling at her nostrils. In minutes, his driving fast, controlled and superb, they arrived at the small village emergency clinic.

For practical purposes it was located adjacent to the public beach where the huge influx of summer visitors didn't always recognize the dangers hidden beneath the benign scene of a perfect summer.

But David knew them. He knew those dangers intimately. Kayla was aware of David's shoulders tightening as he pulled into the parking lot.

He got out of the car and she followed, watching as he went still and gazed out over the nearby beach.

Fried onion and cooking French fries smells wafted out of the concession and the sand was dotted with the yellow-striped sun umbrellas rented from a stand. Out on the water, people who didn't have a clue what they were doing paddled rented kayaks and canoes.

Teenagers had laid claim to the floats that swayed on sparkling waters, and bikini-clad girls shrieked as boys splashed them or tried to toss them in the water.

Toddlers played with sand buckets, mothers handed out sandy potato chips and farther back, among the cottonwoods, grandmothers sat in the deep shade engrossed in books or crossword puzzles.

The lifeguards, alone, were not in fun mode. They sat in high chairs, watching, watching, watching.

She hadn't been there that day it had happened. The day that had changed all of them forever. David was looking at one of the lifeguards, frowning.

What did David see? She saw a young man who was slouched in his chair, looking faintly bored behind sunglasses, as he endlessly scanned the waters between the sand and the buoys that ended the designated swimming area.

For a moment the expression on David's face was unguarded, and she could see sorrow swim in the depths of those amazing eyes. Her animosity toward him flagged. Was it possible that like Kevin, he could not put it behind him?

"David?" She touched his arm.

He broke his gaze and looked at her, momentarily puzzled, as if he didn't know who she was or where he was.

"It was a long time ago," she said softly.

He flinched, and then shook off her arm. "I don't need your pity," he said quietly, his voice cold and hard-edged.

"It wasn't pity," she said, stung.

"What was it, then?" His voice sounded harsh.

She hesitated. "A wish, I guess."

"A wish?"

"That it could somehow be undone. That we could have been the same people we were before it happened."

For a moment he looked like he was going

to say something, and that he bit it back with great effort.

"Wishes are for children," he said grimly.

"And that's the day childhood ended for you," she noted softly.

"No, it isn't. I wasn't a child anymore." He didn't say *neither was Kevin,* but she heard it as clearly as if he had spoken it. "It was the day childhood ended for her. Not us. That little girl who drowned."

"It wasn't your fault."

"No," he said firmly, "It wasn't."

Which left the cold, hard truth about whose fault it had been. It had been an accident. A terrible tragedy.

But somehow he had always blamed Kevin, never forgiven him. David's hard attitude had been part of what destroyed him.

That's what Kayla needed to remember when she was leaning toward him, thinking illicit thoughts about his lips and admiring how posh his car was.

"It was an accident," she said, "There was a full investigation. Ultimately, it was an accident. Her parents should have been watching more closely."

His eyes narrowed on her. "How long did he tell you that before you started believing it?"

"Excuse me?"

His tone was furious. "Her parents weren't trained lifeguards. How would they know that drowning isn't the way it is in the movies? Would they know sometimes there is not a single sound? Not a scream? Not a splash? Not a hand waving frantically in the air?

"He knew that. He knew that, but you know what? He wasn't watching."

Kayla could feel the color draining from her face. "You've always blamed him," she whispered. "Everything changed between the two of you after that. How could you do that? You were his best friend. He needed you."

"He needed to do his job!"

"He was young. He was distracted. Anybody could be distracted for a second."

"The end of our friendship doesn't just fall on my shoulders," David said quietly. "Kevin wouldn't talk to me after the investigation. He was mad because I told the truth."

"What truth?"

He drew in his breath sharply, seemed to consider.

"Tell me," she said, even though she had the childish desire to put her hands over her ears to block what he was going to say next.

"He was flirting with a girl. Instead of doing his job."

She knew David rarely swore, but he inserted an expletive between *his* and *job* that could have made a soldier blush.

"He was over there by the concession not even looking at the water."

"He was already going out with me!" she said, her voice a squeak of outrage and desperation. "That's a lie."

"Is it?" he asked quietly. "I was coming on shift. I wasn't even on duty. I looked out at the water and I knew something was wrong. I could feel it. There was an eeriness in the air. And then I saw that little girl. She had blond hair and she was facedown and her hair floating around her head in the water. I yelled at him as I went by and we both went out."

"You're lying," she whispered again.

He looked at her sadly. "It was too late. By the time we got to her."

"Why would you tell me something so hurtful?" she demanded, but her voice sounded weak in her own ears. "Why would you lie to me like that?"

His eyes were steady on her own.

"Have I ever lied to you, Kayla?" he asked quietly.

"Yes!" she said. "Yes, you have."

And then she turned and practically ran from him before he could see the tears streaming down her face.

CHAPTER FOUR

DAVID'S HAND LANDED on her shoulder, and he spun her around.

"When?" he demanded. "When did I ever lie to you?"

"We kissed that one night on the beach," Kayla said, carefully stripping her voice of any emotion.

His hand fell away from her shoulder, and he stuffed it in the pocket of his shorts and looked away from her.

"And then," she said, her voice a hiss, "you would barely look at me after that. That, David Blaze, is the worst kind of lie of all!"

He drew in his breath, sharply, and looked like he had something to say. Instead, his expression closed.

That same cool, shutting-her-out expression that she remembered all too well from after their ill-fated kiss!

"I don't want to talk about it," he said. "I don't want to talk about any of this."

His tone was dismissive, his eyes that had been so expressive just a moment ago, were guarded. His features were closed and cold, his mouth a firm line that warned her away from the place he did not want to go. Which was their shared history.

And that was not a problem. Because Kayla didn't want to go there, either.

"You brought it up," she reminded him tightly.

He scraped a hand though his hair and sighed, a sound heavy with weariness. "I did. I shouldn't have. I'm sorry."

"Thank you for your help," Kayla said with stiff formality. "I can take it from here. I've taken enough of your time. You should go."

David was aware Kayla was taking her cues from him. Slamming the door shut on their shared past.

David was aware he had managed to hurt her feelings, and make her very angry and he was genuinely sorry for both.

Her husband was dead. What momentary and completely uncharacteristic lack of control had made him tell her, after all these years, about what had happened that day?

He supposed it was because she had taken

Kevin's word and way, absolved him of responsibility by blaming those poor parents, as innocent in the whole thing as their child had been.

The drowning *had* been ruled an accident. But the tension between him and Kevin had never been repaired.

It was only the fact that he had just saved Kayla's life that was making her struggle for even a modicum of courtesy. In other circumstances, David was aware that he probably would have found that struggle, so transparent in her face and eyes, somewhat amusing.

You should go. That was a good idea if David had ever heard one.

He still could not believe the anger he felt when she said that about it being the parents' responsibility, his anger at how completely she had bought into Kevin absolving himself.

Still, it *was* all a long time ago. Her voice saying that, soft with compassion, was something worth escaping from.

It *was* a long time ago.

Sometimes months could go by without him thinking of it.

But that was not while looking at the beach, with Kayla at his side. He didn't like it that she had seen, instantly, that it still bothered him.

And he liked it even less that her hand had

rested on his wrist, her touch gentle and offering understanding.

Kayla. Some things never changed. She was always looking for something or someone to save, Kevin being a case in point.

Kevin had died in a car accident on a slippery night, going too fast, as always. Had he not cared that he had responsibilities? The accident had happened very late at night. Why hadn't he been home with his beautiful, young wife?

David shook it off. It was none of his business, but he wished she had not brought up that kiss. He remembered every single thing about it: the sand of the day clinging to them both, the bonfire, the sky star-studded and inky, the night air warm and sultry, the velvety softness of her cheek nestled into his hand as she gazed at him with those huge, liquid-green eyes. His lips had been pulled to her lips like steel to a magnet. And when he had tasted them, they had tasted sweetly of the nectar that gave life.

Until that precise moment, that electrifying meeting of lips, they had just been friends in a circle of friends. But they had been at that age when awareness is sharpening...where the potential for everything to change is always shimmering in the air.

It was true. What he had done after was the worst kind of lie.

Because the next day, Kevin, who had not been at the bonfire the night before, had told David *he* had fallen for Kayla. That he'd known forever that she was the girl for him, that he had asked her to the prom and she had said yes.

Obviously, Kevin had asked her to the prom before David had kissed her.

He'd felt the dilemma of it; his best friend was staking a claim, *had* a prior claim. Since his own father had died, David had practically lived at the house next door. He and Kevin were more than friends. They were brothers. Plus, what had Kayla been doing kissing David when she'd agreed to go with Kevin to the prom?

David had done the only possible thing. He'd backed off. In truth, he had probably thought he might have another chance to explore the electricity that had leaped so spontaneously between him and Kayla.

He had thought the thing between her and Kevin would play itself out. Kevin never stuck with anything for long.

But then the little girl had drowned. On Kevin's watch. And the days of that summer had become a swiftly churning kaleidoscope that they all had been sucked into. A kaleidoscope of loss and of pain and guilt and remorse and sadness. And of anger.

And somehow, when the kaleidoscope had stopped spinning and had spit them all out, Kayla and Kevin were engaged.

It occurred to David that he had been angry at Kevin long before that child had drowned.

"You need to go."

Kayla said it again, more firmly.

David wanted to get away from her, and from the anger in her eyes, and the recrimination, and the pain that shaded the green to something deeper than green.

She dismissed him, turning her back on him, marching through the doors of the clinic.

The easiest thing would have been to let her go.

But when had David ever done what was easy?

He had promised to see to her dog and her things, and the fact that his word was solid gold was part of what had allowed him to go so far in the world. Blaze Enterprises had been built on a concept of integrity that was rare in the business world.

He followed her through the doors of the clinic.

The ancient nurse, Mary McIntyre, insisted that Kayla take one of the beds in the empty clinic, and so, even though Kayla had dismissed him, he followed them as Mary fussed around her, asking questions, taking her pulse and her blood pressure and listening to her heart.

"We'll just keep an eye on you, dear. There's a doctor three minutes away if we need him."

"Okay," Kayla said, settled on the cot, her arms folded across her chest. She glared at David. "Why are you still here?"

"Just making sure."

She raised a comically puffy eyebrow at him. "You don't need my pity. I don't need your help. I'm chaperoned. I can't possibly get into any more trouble. The neighborhood kids are out looking for my dog and are retrieving my purse, so you can go."

It was like coming through a smoky building fraught with danger, and finally catching sight of the red exit sign.

"Do you want me to pick you up in a couple of hours?"

David contemplated the words that had just come out of his mouth, astounded. He wasn't even planning on being here in a couple of hours. A quick check on his mother, a consult with her care aides and gone.

The urgency to get back to *his* world felt intense.

Especially now that he'd had this run-in with Kayla.

But in a moment of madness he had promised to look after her dog, and bike and purse. He had tangled their lives together for a little while longer. But escape was just postponed, not canceled.

And apparently, she was just as eager not to tangle their lives as he was.

"I've got the neighborhood kids on the case of my dog. I mean it would be nice if you checked, but no, don't feel obligated. And no, definitely don't come back. I'll just walk home. It's not far."

She had been riding her bike on Sugar Maple. Did she live close to there?

"Where are you staying?"

She gave him a puzzled look. "I thought your mom would have told you."

"Told me what?" he said cautiously.

His mother, these days, told him lots of things. That someone was sneaking into the house stealing her eyeglasses. And wine decanters. That she'd had the nicest conversation with his father, who had been dead for seventeen years.

That was part of the reason he was here.

One of the live-in care aides had called him late last night and said, in the careful undertone of one who might be listened to, *You should come. It may not be safe for her to be at home anymore.*

He had known it was coming, and yet been shocked by it all the same. Wasn't he back in his hometown hoping it was an overreaction? That if he just hired more staff he would not have to take his mother from the only home she had known for the past forty years?

It seemed to David, of all the losses that this town had handed him, this was the biggest one of all.

He was losing his mother. But he was not confiding that in Kayla, with her all-too-ready sympathy!

"You thought my mother would tell me where you lived?"

"David, I'm her next-door neighbor."

His mouth fell open and he forced it shut. That was a rather large oversight on his mother's part.

"The house was too much for Kevin's folks," Kayla said.

He'd known that. The house had been empty the last few times he had visited; he had noticed the Jaffreys were no longer there the next time he'd returned to Blossom Valley after Kevin's funeral. It probably wasn't the house that was too much, but the memories it contained.

David had his fair share of those, too. He'd

felt a sense of loss, to go with his growing string of losses that he felt when he came home, at seeing the house empty. He had practically grown up in that house next door to his, he and Kevin passing in and out of each other's kitchens since they were toddlers.

Both of them had been only children, and maybe that was why they had become brothers to each other as much as friends.

There was no part of David's childhood that did not have Kevin in it. He was part of the fabric of every Christmas and birthday. They had learned to ride two-wheelers and strapped on their first skates together. They had shared the first day of school. They had chosen David's puppy together, and the dog that had been on their heels all the days of their youth had really belonged to both of them.

They had built the tree fort in Kevin's backyard, and swam across the bay together every single summer.

When David's dad had died, Mr. Jaffrey had acted like a father to both of them.

No, maybe not a father. More like a friend. Had that been part of the problem with Kevin? A problem David had successfully ignored for years?

No rules. No firm hand. No guidelines. An only child, totally indulged, who had, despite his fun-loving charm, become increasingly self-centered.

The Jaffreys' empty house had looked more forlorn with each visit: paint needing freshening up, shingles curling, porch sagging, yard overgrown.

That house had once been so full of love and laughter and hopes and dreams. The state it was in now made it seem like the final few words in the closing chapter of a book with a sad ending.

David wondered if maybe the reason he had stayed so angry at Kevin was because if he ever let go of that, the sadness would swallow him whole.

"The Jaffreys got a condo on the water," Kayla continued. "The house would have gone to Kevin, eventually. They wanted me to have it."

He let that sink in. Kayla was his mother's next-door neighbor. She was living in the house he and Kevin had chased through in those glorious, carefree days of their youth.

He didn't want to ask her anything. He didn't want to know.

And yet he annoyed himself by asking anyway, "Doesn't that house need quite a lot of work?"

He hoped she would hear his lack of enthusiasm. And he thought he caught a momentary glimpse of the fact she was overwhelmed by the house in something faintly worried in her eyes. But she covered it quickly.

"Yes!" she said, her enthusiasm striking him as faintly forced. "It needs everything."

Naturally, she would never walk away from that particular gift horse. She was *needed*.

He couldn't stop himself. "Do you ever give up on hopeless causes?"

CHAPTER FIVE

KAYLA LOOKED BRIEFLY WOUNDED and then she just looked mad. David liked her angry look quite a bit better than the wounded one. The wounded expression made her look vulnerable and made him feel protective of her, even though he had caused it in the first place!

"Are you talking about the house?" she asked dangerously.

He answered safely, "Yes," though he was aware, as was she, that he could have been talking about Kevin.

"Do you ever get tired of being a wet blanket?"

"I prefer to think of it as being the voice of reason."

"I don't care to hear it."

David didn't care what Kayla cared to hear. She obviously was in for some hard truths today, whether she liked it or not. Maybe somebody did have to protect her. From herself! And apparently, no one had stepped up to the plate to do that so far.

"That house," he said, his tone cool and reasonable, "is doing a long, slow slide into complete ruin."

"It isn't," she said, as though he hadn't been reasonable at all. "And it isn't a hopeless cause!"

There. He'd said his piece. Despite the fact that he dealt in investments, including real estate, all the time, his expertise had been rejected.

He could leave with a clear conscience. He had tried to warn her away from a house that was a little more—a lot more—of a project than any thinking person would take on, let alone a single woman.

"I've already ordered all new windows," she said stubbornly. "And the floors are scheduled for refinishing."

A money pit, he thought to himself. He ordered himself to shut up, so was astounded when, out loud, he said drily, "Kayla to the rescue."

She frowned at him.

Stop! David yelled at himself. But he didn't stop. "I bet the dog is a rescue, too, isn't it?"

He had his answer when she flushed. He realized Kevin wasn't the only one he was angry with.

"There was quite a large insurance settlement," she said, her voice stiff with pride. "Can you think of a better use for it than restoring Kevin's childhood home?"

"Actually, yes."

She was in his field of expertise now. This is what he did, and he did it extremely well. He counseled people on how to invest their money. Blaze Enterprises was considered one of the most successful investment firms in Canada.

"A falling-down house in Blossom Valley would probably rate dead last on my list of potential places to put money."

"Are you always so crushingly practical?"

"Yes."

"Humph. Well, I'm going to buy a business here, too," she said stubbornly, her swollen brows drawing together as she read his lack of elaboration for what it was: a complete lack of enthusiasm.

"Really?" he said, not even trying to hide the cynical note from his voice.

"Really," she shot back. Predictably, his cynicism was only making her dig in even deeper. "I'm looking at an ice cream parlor."

"An ice cream parlor? Hmm, that just edged the house out of the position of dead last on my list of potential investments," he said drily.

"More-moo is for sale," she said, as though she hadn't heard him. "On Main Street."

As if the location would change his mind.

He told himself he didn't care how she spent her money. Didn't care if she blew the whole wad.

But somehow he did. Given free rein, Kayla would rescue the world until there was not a single crumb left for herself.

There was no doubt in his mind that More-moo was one more rescue for her, one more thing destined for failure and therefore irresistible. It was time for him to walk away. And yet he thought if he did not try to dissuade her he might not be able to sleep at night.

Sleep was important.

"Nobody sells a business at the top of its game," he cautioned her.

"The owners are retiring."

"Uh-huh."

She looked even more stubborn, her attempts to furrow her brow thwarted somewhat by how swollen it was.

It was none of his business. Let her throw her money around until she had none left.

But of course, that was the problem with having tasted her lips all those years ago. And it was the problem with having chased with her through endless summers on the lake. It was the problem with having studied with her for exams, and walked to school with her on crisp fall days, and sat beside her at the movies, their buttered fingers accidentally touching over popcorn.

It was the problem with having surrendered the first girl he had ever cared about to his best friend, only to watch catastrophe unfold.

There was a feeling that he had dropped the ball, maybe when it mattered most. He couldn't set back the clock. But maybe he could manage not to drop the ball this time.

Whether he wanted to or not, David had a certain emotional attachment to her—whether he wanted to or not, he cared what happened to her.

At least he could set Kayla straight on the ice cream parlor.

"There is no way," he said with elaborate patience, "to make money at a business where you only have good numbers for eight weeks of the year. You've seen this town in the winter. And spring, and fall, for that matter. You could shoot off a cannon on Main Street and not hit anyone."

"The demographics are changing," she said, as if she hoped he would be impressed by her use of the word *demographics*. "People are living here all year round. It's become quite a retirement choice."

"It's still a business that will only ever have eight good weeks every year. And even those eight weeks are weather dependent. Nobody eats ice cream in the rain."

"We did," she said softly.

"Huh?"

"We did. We ate ice cream in the rain."

David frowned. And then he remembered a sudden thunderstorm on a hot afternoon. Maybe they had been sixteen? Certainly it had been the summer before the kaleidoscope, before he had kissed her, before Kevin had laid claim, before the drowning.

A group of them had been riding their bikes down Main Street and had been caught out by the suddenness of the storm.

It had felt thrilling riding through the slashing rain and flashing lightning, until they had taken cover under the awning of the ice cream store as the skies turned black and the thunder rolled around them.

How could he possibly remember that Kayla's T-shirt had been soaked through and had become transparent, showing the details of a surprisingly sexy bra, and that Cedric Parson had been sneaking peeks?

So David had taken his own shirt off and

pulled it over Kayla's head, making her still wetter, but not transparently so. He could even remember the feeling: standing under that awning on Main Street, bare chested, David had felt manly and protective instead of faintly ridiculous and cold.

How could he possibly remember that he'd had black ice cream, licorice flavored? And that her tongue had darted out of her mouth and mischievously licked a drip from his cone? And that he had deliberately placed his lips where her tongue had been?

How could he possibly remember that he had felt like the electricity in the air had sizzled deep inside him, and that ice cream had never since tasted as good as it had that electric afternoon?

David shook off the memory and the seductive power it had to make him think maybe people would eat ice cream in the rain.

"Generally speaking, people are not going to go for ice cream if the weather is bad," he said practically. "One season of bad weather, you'd be finished. A few days of bad weather would probably put an ice cream parlor close to the edge."

"Well, I like the idea of owning an ice cream parlor," Kayla said firmly. "I like it a lot."

He took in her eyes peering at him stubbornly from under her comically swollen forehead, and knew this wasn't the time.

"Your ambition in life is to be up to your elbows, digging through vats of frozen-solid ice cream until your hands cramp?"

"That sounds like I'm selling a lot of ice cream," she purred with satisfaction.

"Humph."

"My ambition," she told him, something faintly dangerous in her tone, "is to make people happy. What makes anyone happier than ice cream on a hot day?"

Or during a thunderstorm, his own mind filled in, unbidden.

He said, "Humph," again, more emphatically than the last time.

"It's a simple pleasure," she said stubbornly. "The world needs more of those. Way more."

He had a feeling if he wanted to convince Kayla, he had better back his argument with hard, cold facts: graphs and projections and five years' worth of More-moo's financial statements. What would it hurt to have one of his assistants do a bit of research?

"I would like to bring in specialty ice creams. Did you know, in the Middle East, rose petal ice cream is a big hit?"

He felt she had already given her ice cream

parlor dreams way more thought than they deserved.

David was pretty sure he felt the beginnings of a headache throbbing along the line of his forehead and into his temples.

"I bet people would drive here from Toronto for rose petal ice cream," she said dreamily.

David stared at her. She couldn't possibly believe that! Why did he feel as if he needed to personally dissuade her from unrealistic dreams?

Because he had failed to do so when it had really mattered.

Don't marry him, Kayla.

Tears streaming down her face. "I have to."

He could only guess what that fateful decision had put her through. He was going to guess that being married to Kevin had been no bed of roses. Or rose petals, either.

And yet here she was, still dreaming. Was there a certain kind of courage in that?

He hated coming home.

"I'll go see how the kids are doing with finding the dog," David said gruffly.

He could clearly see she wanted to refuse this offer—a warning she wasn't exactly going to embrace his unsolicited advice about the ice cream parlor with open arms—but her concern for the little beast won out.

"You have a cell?" he asked her.

"In pieces on the road, probably," she said wryly.

"I'll call here to the clinic, then, when I find out about the dog. Is he a certain breed?"

"Why?"

"If the kids haven't found him, or I don't find him hiding under a shrub near where you got stung, I'll find a picture on the internet and have my assistant, Jane, make a poster. She can email it to me, and I'll have it printed here."

Under her comical brows, Kayla was transparent. She was both annoyed by his ability to take charge and his organizational skills, and relieved by them, too. No doubt it would be the same reaction when he presented her with the total lack of viability for operating an ice cream parlor in Blossom Valley.

"He's a toy Brussels Griffon," she said, hopeful that he would find the dog, yet reluctant to enlist his aid and hating that she was relying on him. But Kayla was as emotional as he was analytical, her every situation driven by her heart instead of her head.

He put it into his phone. A picture of the world's ugliest dog materialized, big eyes, wiry hair popping out in all the wrong places. The hair springing from the dog's ears and above his eyes reminded him of an old man, badly in need of an eyebrow and ear trim.

"Is it just me, or does this dog bear a resemblance to Einstein?" he muttered, showing her the picture.

"Hence the name," she said, and he smiled reluctantly. Damned if the dog didn't bear a striking resemblance to the high school teacher, Mr. Bastigal, who had emulated his science hero right down to the crazy gray hair and walrus mustache.

When she nodded that the dog on the screen resembled hers, he slipped the phone into his pocket and vowed to himself he would find it. He ran a multimillion-dollar empire. Troubleshooting was his specialty. One small dog was no match for him. It *looked* like Einstein. That didn't mean it was smart.

And while he was tracking down the doggie, an assistant could do the homework on Moremoo, not that it mattered. He was willing to bet Kayla would find another failing business to ride to the rescue of once she was given the reality check on More-moo.

"I'll leave Mary a business card with my cell number on it. You can call me if you change your mind about the ride home."

"I won't."

He scanned her face, nodded and left the

room, leaving the card with Mary, as promised. Mary seemed to want to catch up—she'd been the nurse here way back when he was lifeguarding, and she'd seemed old then—but he begged off, claiming responsibility for the dog.

David Blaze had had enough of old home week. Except, as he walked back out into the sultry heat of the July day, he glanced at his watch. He hadn't been here a week. Nowhere near. It had been thirty-two whole minutes since he had last checked his watch in the snarled traffic of Main Street.

CHAPTER SIX

KAYLA WAS AT HOME, and in bed. She could not sleep. She ordered herself not to look at the bedside alarm, but she did, anyway.

It was 3:10 a.m.

She was exhausted, and wide awake at the same time, possibly from the drugs in her system.

But possibly sleep eluded her because she had become used to her little dog cuddled against her in the night, his sweet snores, his wiry whiskers tickling her chin, his eyes popping open to make sure she was still there, staring deeply at her, his liquid gaze holding nothing but devotion and loyalty.

Unlike her husband.

Wasn't that why she was really awake? Contemplating what David had told her about the day of the drowning?

She had called David a liar.

But in her heart, she had felt the sickening reverberation of truth.

That, Kayla decided, was what was hateful about being awake at this time of night. She was held hostage by the thoughts that she could fend off during the day. During the day there was so much this old house needed, it was overwhelming.

But being overwhelmed was not necessarily a bad thing. It could occupy her every thought and every waking hour. Between that, the new dog and looking for the perfect investment opportunity, she was blessedly busy.

But on a night like tonight, thoughts crowded into her tired mind. Even before David had said that about Kevin flirting with a girl instead of doing his job, Kayla had lain awake at night and contemplated her marriage.

She tried to direct her thoughts to good things and good memories, like the night he had proposed, so sweet and serious and sincere.

I want to do the honorable thing. For once.

She frowned. She hadn't thought of that part of it for a long time, and not in the light she was thinking of it now. Had he loved her, or had he done the honorable thing?

Crazy thoughts. Middle of the night thoughts. Of course he had loved her.

In his way. So what if his way bought flowers when they needed groceries? That was romantic! And he had been a dreamer. That was a good memory. Of them sitting at the kitchen table, in the early days of their marriage sipping the last of their coffee, his face all intense and earnest as he described what he wanted for them: a business of their own, a big house, a great car.

Disloyal to think his dreams had been grandiose and made it impossible for him to settle for an ordinary life. Within days of finding a job, it would seem his litany of complaints would begin. He wasn't appreciated. He wasn't being paid enough. His boss was a jerk. His coworkers were inferior, his great ideas weren't being listened to or implemented.

She never stopped hoping and praying that he would find himself, that he would grow up to be a man with all the best characteristics of that boy she had grown up with—so fun-loving and energetic and full of mischief.

Kevin had rewarded her unflagging belief in him by increasingly taking her for granted. He had become careless of her feelings—though the old charm would return, temporarily, when she threatened to leave or when it managed to bail them out of one of his predicaments yet again.

The old charm. The one thing he was good

at. What had David meant about Kevin flirting with a girl? Had he been talking to her? Or more? Touching her? Kissing her?

Had Kevin had affairs during their marriage?

There. She was there, at the place she had refused to go since her husband's death. It felt like she had just plunged into a hard place at the core of her, that did not go away because she pretended it was not there, that had not been a part of her makeup before she had married Kevin.

Was it this very suspicion that had caused it? This suspicion, and *so* much disappointment that it felt so disloyal to look at?

She had wondered about Kevin's fidelity even before David's shocking revelation outside of the clinic that afternoon. It seemed to her the more Kevin failed at everything else, the more she had become lonely within their marriage, the more he had exercised his substantial charm outside of it.

Where had he been, when speeding toward home too late at night, the car sliding on ice and slamming into a tree?

No seat belt. So like Kevin.

He had been chronically irresponsible, and others had picked up the tab for that.

It felt like David's fault, David's sudden unexpected presence in her life, and his revelations of this afternoon that had brought these thoughts, lurking beneath the surface, surging to the top.

Kayla blinked back tears. It had just all gone so terribly, terribly wrong. The tears felt weak, and at the same time, better than that hard, cold rock she carried around where her heart used to be.

And now David was back, and words she had not allowed herself to think of in those five long years of marriage to Kevin were at the forefront of her mind.

Don't marry him, Kayla.

She considered the awful possibility that David, who had withheld his forgiveness, had not been the cause of Kevin's downward spiral, but that he had seen something about his oldest friend that she had missed.

And who was withholding forgiveness now? It was pathetic. But now that her feelings had surfaced, she was aware one of them was anger. It was useless to feel that way. Kevin was dead. It could never be fixed.

"Stop it," Kayla ordered herself, but instead she thought of how David's hand had felt on her thigh, how she had leaned toward him, wanting, if she had only seconds left, one last taste of him.

Those thoughts made her feel restless, and hungry with a hunger that a midnight snack would never be able to fill.

Irritated with the ruminations of an exhausted mind, she yanked off the sheet that covered her, sat up and swung her legs out of the bed.

She padded over to her open window, where old-fashioned chintz curtains danced slowly on a cooling summer breeze. The window coverings throughout the house were thirty years behind the current styles, and one more thing on the long "to-do" list.

Which Kayla also didn't want to be thinking about in the dead of night, a time when things could become overwhelming.

She diverted herself, squinting hopefully at her backyard. The moon was out and bright, but the massive, mature sugar maple at the center of the yard, and overgrown shrub beds, where peonies and forsythia competed with weeds, cast most of the yard in deep shadow where a small dog could hide.

Her little dog was out there somewhere. She had no doubt he was afraid. Poor little Bastigal was afraid of everything: loud noises and quick movements, and men and cats and the wind in leaves.

It was probably what was making him so

hard to find. All afternoon he had probably been quivering under a shrub, hidden as the hordes of Blossom Valley children ran by, calling his name.

And it was hordes.

Walking home from the clinic there had been a poster on every telephone pole, with a picture of a Brussels Griffon on it that looked amazingly like Bastigal.

Under it had been the promise of a five-hundred dollar reward for his return.

And *David's* cell phone number. Well, she could hardly resent that. Her own cell phone had been left with her bicycle, her purse, her hat and her crushed sunflowers on her front porch. Blossom Valley being Blossom Valley, her purse was undisturbed, all her credit cards and cash still in it. But her cell phone had been shattered beyond repair, and since she had opted not to have a landline, it was the only phone she had.

So she could not resent the use of his number, but she did resent the reward. Obviously, she could not allow him to pay it, and obviously she did not have an extra five hundred dollars lying around. It hadn't been a good idea, anyway. She had no doubt the enthusiasm of the children, reward egging them on like a carrot on a stick before a donkey, was frightening her dog into deeper hiding.

She looked out the window, willing herself to see through the inky darkness. Was it possible Bastigal would have found his way to his own yard? Would he recognize this as his own yard? They'd only been back in Blossom Valley, in their new home, for a little over two weeks. She hadn't even finished unpacking boxes yet.

But through the open window, Kayla thought she heard the faintest sound coming from between the houses, and her heart leaped.

Grabbing a light sweater off the hook behind her closet door, glad to have an urgent purpose that would help her to escape her own thoughts, Kayla moved through her darkened, and still faintly unfamiliar, house and out the back door into her yard.

Hers.

Despite the loss of the dog and her undisciplined thoughts of earlier, the feeling of having a place of her own to call home calmed something in her.

She became aware it was a beautiful night, and her yard looked faintly magical in the moonlight, not showing neglect as it did in the harsh light of day. It was easy to overlook the fact the grass needed mowing and just appreciate that it was thick and dewy under her feet.

There was a scent in the air that was cool and pure and invigorating.

She heard, again, some slight noise around the corner of her house, and her heart jumped. Bastigal. He had come home after all!

She rounded the corner of her house, and stopped short.

"Mrs. Blaze?"

David's mother turned her head and looked at her, smiling curiously. And yet the smile did not hide a certain vacant look in her eyes. She was in a nightgown that had not been buttoned down the front. She also wore a straw gardening hat, and bright pink winter boots. She was holding pruning shears, and a pile of thorny branches were accumulating at her feet.

Kayla noticed several scratches on her arms were bleeding.

It occurred to her she hadn't really seen Mrs. Blaze since taking up residence next door. She had meant to go over and say hello when her boxes were unpacked.

In a glance she could see why David's mother had not told him who had moved in next door. She was fairly certain she was not recognized by the woman who had known Kayla's husband all of his life, and Kayla for a great deal of hers.

"It's me," Kayla said, gently. "Kayla Jaffrey."

Mrs. Blaze frowned and turned back to the

roses. She snapped the blades of the pruners at a branch and missed.

"It used to be McIntosh. I'm friends with your son, David." *Why did I say that, instead of that I was Kevin's wife?*

Not that it mattered. Mrs. Blaze cast her a look that was totally bewildered. A deep sadness opened up in Kayla as she realized she was not the only one in Blossom Valley dealing with major and devastating life changes.

She stepped carefully around the thorny branches, plucked the dangerously waving pruners from Mrs. Blaze's hands and set them on the ground. She shrugged out of her sweater and tucked it lightly around Mrs. Blaze's shoulders, buttoning it quickly over the gaping nightie.

"Let's get you home, shall we?" Kayla offered her elbow.

"But the roses…"

"I'll look after them," Kayla promised.

"I don't know. I like to do it myself. The gardener can't be trusted. If roses aren't properly pruned…" Her voice faded, troubled, as if she was struggling to recall what would happen if the roses weren't properly pruned.

"I'll look after them," Kayla promised again.

"Oh. I suppose. Are you a gardener?"

What was the harm in one little white lie? "Yes."

"Don't forget the pruners, then," Mrs. Blaze snapped, and Kayla saw a desperate need to be in control in the sharpness of the command.

She stooped and picked up the pruners, then took advantage of the budding trust in Mrs. Blaze's eyes to offer her elbow again. This time Mrs. Blaze threaded her fragile arm through Kayla's and allowed Kayla to guide her through the small wedge of land that separated the two properties. They went through the open gate into the Blaze yard.

Kayla had assumed, looking over her fence at it, that Mrs. Blaze gardened. The lawn was manicured, the beds filled with flowers and dark loam, weed free. Now she realized there must be the gardener Mrs. Blaze had referred to.

Kayla led David's mother up the stairs and onto the back veranda. Again, she had been admiring it from her own yard. Everything here was beautifully maintained: the expansive deck newly stained, beautiful, inviting furniture scattered over its surface, potted plants spilling an abundance of color and fragrance.

She had been holding out the hope her own property was going to look like this one day. Now she wondered just how much time—or staff—it took to make a place look this perfect. Once she had her own business, would she be able to manage it? She tried not to let the thought make her feel deflated.

Kayla knocked at the door, lightly, and when nothing happened, louder. She was just about to put her head in the door and call out when from within the house she heard the sound of feet coming down the stairs.

She knew from the sound of the tread it was likely David—and who else would it be after all—but still, she did not feel prepared when the door was flung open.

David Blaze stood there, half-asleep and half-naked, unconsciously and mouthwateringly sexy, looking about as magnificent as a man could look.

CHAPTER SEVEN

DAVID'S CHOCOLATE HAIR was sleep tousled, and his dark eyes held faint, dazed amusement as he gazed at the two nightie-clad women in front of him.

Kayla gazed back. He stood there in only a pair of blue-plaid pajama pants that hung dangerously low over the faint jut of his hips.

He didn't have on anything else. His body was magnificent. He was deeper and broader than he had been all those years ago when he had been a lifeguard. The boyish sleekness of his muscle had deepened into the powerful build of a man in his prime. There was not an ounce of superfluous flesh on him.

In the darkness of the night he looked as if he had been carved from alabaster: beautiful shoulders, carved, smooth chest, washboard abs on his stomach.

Kayla gulped.

David came full awake, and the faint amusement was doused in his eyes as he took them both in, lingering on Kayla's own nightie-clad self a second more than necessary. It occurred to her the nightie, light as it was and perfect for hot summer nights, was just a little sheer for this kind of encounter. Her shoulders felt suddenly too bare, and she could feel cool air on the thighs that had already been way too exposed to him.

David seemed to draw his eyes away from her reluctantly. Kayla could feel her pulse hammering in the hollow of her throat.

"Mom," he said gently, swinging open the screen door, "come in the house."

His mother looked at him searchingly and then her expression tightened. "I don't know who you are," she snapped, "but don't think I don't know my wallet is missing."

"We'll find your wallet." His voice was measured, and the tone remained gentle. But Kayla saw the enormous pain that darkened his eyes as his mother moved toward him.

"And the roses need pruning," Mrs. Blaze snapped at her son.

He winced, and at that moment, a woman came up behind them, dressed in a white uniform.

"Mr. Blaze, I'm so sorry. I—"

He gave her a look that said he didn't want

to hear it, and passed his mother into her care. "It looks like she has some scratches on her arms, if you could tend to those."

"Yes, sir."

There was something faintly shocking about hearing David—the boy who had romped through the days of summer with her, and played tricks on their teachers, and sat in with her at bonfires licking marshmallow off his fingers—addressed in such a deferential tone of voice.

The door shut behind his mother and the care aide, and he stepped out onto the porch. His face was composed, but Kayla saw him draw in a deep, steadying breath, and then another.

It filled his chest and drew her eyes to the masculine perfection of that surface.

"Thank you," he said quietly. "Where was she?"

Her eyes skittered away from his chest, and to his face. The lateness of the hour and the pain in his face made all the hurts between them seem less important somehow. She found that she wanted to reach up and ease the stern, worried lines that had creased around his mouth.

"In my yard, pruning the roses." Kayla handed him the pruning shears, and he took them and stared down at them for a moment, then looked out at the garden shed, the door hanging open.

"I guess that needs to be locked," he said.

"I didn't know," Kayla said softly. "I haven't been over yet since I got back. The house and yard looked so beautifully maintained, I just assumed your mom was going as strong as ever."

"One of my property managers makes sure the maintenance gets done, and the yard is looked after." He looked around sadly. "It does look like normal people live here, doesn't it?"

"I'm so sorry, David," she said softly, and then again, "I didn't know."

He smiled a little tightly. "No pity," he warned her.

"It wasn't pity," she said, a little hotly.

"What, then?"

"It was compassion."

"Ah." He didn't look convinced, or any more willing to accept whatever she was offering no matter what name she put on it. "What are you doing out here, anyway? What time is it?"

"After three." No sense confessing all the terrible thoughts that had kept her from sleeping. "I was worried about my dog. I couldn't sleep. I heard a noise out here and thought it might be Bastigal."

"And it was Mom. It's a mercy that you

found her before she wandered off or hurt herself with the pruners." He shook his head. "She can't remember what she had for breakfast—"

Or her own son, Kayla thought sadly.

"—but she worked her way past two security locks, a dead bolt and a childproof handle on the door."

Kayla was afraid to tell him, again, how sorry she was.

"There's a live-in aide, but obviously she was distracted by something. I think she sneaks the odd cigarette out here on the deck. Maybe she left the door open behind her."

Kayla shivered a little at his tone, very happy she was not in the aide's shoes.

"How long has your mom been like that?" Kayla asked softly.

It looked like a conversation he didn't want to have, but then he sighed, as if it was a surrender to confide in her.

"She's been deteriorating for a couple of years," he said softly. "It starts so small you can overlook it, or wish it away. I'd notice things when I visited: toothpaste in the refrigerator, mismatching socks, saying the same thing she just said. When I wasn't here, she'd phone me. She lost the car. Where was Dad? That was when she could still remember my phone number."

David stopped abruptly, took a deep breath, as if he was shaking off the need to confide. His voice cooled. "I've had live-in help for her for nearly two months. The last few weeks, the decline has seemed more rapid. I don't think she's going to be able to stay here any longer."

So what could she say, if not "sorry"? But Kayla had dealt with her own grief, and sometimes she knew how words, intended to help, could just increase the feeling of being lonely and alone.

Instead of words she reached out and placed her palm over his heart. She wasn't even sure why. Perhaps to let him know she could feel it breaking?

His skin felt beautiful under her fingertips, like silk that had been warmed in the sun. And his heartbeat was steady and strong. She didn't know if the gesture comforted him, but it did her. She could feel his strength, and knew he had enough of it to cope with whatever came next.

For a moment he stood gazing down at her hand, transfixed. And then he covered it with his own.

Something more powerful than words passed between them, and she felt a shiver of something for David she had not felt ever before.

Certainly not with her own husband.

Shaken, and trying desperately not to show it, she withdrew her hand from under the warm, resilient promise of his.

For a moment, an electric silence ran between them. Then David ran his freed hand through the crisp darkness of his hair. "No dog, I assume?"

Kayla was inordinately relieved at the change of subject, at the words sliding like cooling raindrops into the place that sizzled like an electrical storm between them. "No. I hoped he might have found his way back to the yard."

"I'm sorry I didn't find him."

"It's not for lack of trying. Thank you for the posters—they brought out an army of children. I'll reimburse you, of course."

He shrugged. "Whatever."

"And naturally, I'll pay the reward when we find him."

"It's okay, Kayla. I offered it, I'll pay it."

"No."

"It's probably a moot point, anyway."

"You think we aren't going to find him?" she asked, trying to keep the panic from her voice. David obviously had bigger things to think about than her dog.

"Oh, I think you'll find him. I just don't think the kids will. He's a timid little guy, isn't he?"

"Yes. How did you know?"

"Well, I saw him scurry away after he fell out of the basket when you got stung."

"Did he look hurt?"

"Not at the rate he was running, no. I had spotted you before that. Riding down Main Street. Even then the dog had a distinctly worried look on his face."

Despite herself, she chuckled. "That's him—my little worrier. I'll probably never get him to ride in the basket again!"

"A pair well matched. You're both worriers!"

To be standing with such a gorgeous man and pegged as a worrier! What did she want to be seen as? Carefree? Lively? Happy?

But David always saw straight to the heart of things, and the last few years of her life had been rife with worry. Kayla self-consciously touched her brow, wondering if there was a permanent mark of it there.

Thankfully, David was scanning the bushes. "I don't think he's going to come out for the reward-hungry children running through the streets shrieking his name. Sorry. A misstep on my part."

"He'll show up," she said, but she could hear the wistfulness—and worry—in her own voice.

"I hope so." She knew she should say goodnight and leave his porch, cross the little strip of grass that separated their properties and close the gate firmly between them.

But she didn't.

When had she become this lonely? She felt like she ached for his company. Anyone's company, probably. She didn't want to return to that empty house, the wayward direction of her restless thoughts.

He was looking at her, smiling slightly.

"What?"

"There is a quality about you that begs to be painted."

"What?" She wanted to press her brow again!

"I noticed it when I saw you on the bike. I could almost see a painting of you—Girl on a Bicycle.

"And now, out here in your white nightdress on the porch. Girl on a Summer Night." He shrugged, embarrassed.

But she felt as if she drank in the words like a flower deprived too long of water.

In that *Lakeside Life* feature on David and Blaze Enterprises, it had said, almost as an aside, that David had one of the largest private collections of art in the country. Again, the man who stood in front of her did not seem like the same boy who had raced her on bicycles down these tree-lined streets.

This David, this man of the world and collector of art, thought she was worthy of a painting? He saw something else in her besides a furrow-browed worrier?

Kayla could feel tears smarting her eyes, so she said swiftly, carelessly, turning her head from his gaze and pressing her fingers into her forehead to erase any remaining worry lines, "I guess the swelling has gone down, then." She pretended she was concerned about the swelling from the beesting rather than the worry lines!

She felt his fingers on her chin, turning her unwilling gaze back to him.

He searched her face, and she felt as if she was wide open to him: the loneliness, the crushing disappointment, the constant worry, all of it. She felt as if he could see her.

And she realized, stunned, she had always felt like that. As if David could see her.

The longing that leaped within her terrified her. The longing and the recrimination. She suddenly felt as if every choice she had ever made had been wrong.

And she probably still could not be trusted with choices!

Kayla reminded herself she had made a vow that she was not going to offer herself on the altar of love anymore.

She had vowed to be content with the house

Kevin's parents had given her—restoring it to some semblance of order, never mind its former glory, should be enough to fill her days! Add to that her dog, when she found him, and eventually her business when she discovered the right one.

Those things would fill her, complete her, give her purpose, without leaving her open to the pain and heartache of loving.

She hated it that the night was working some odd magic on her, that she would even think the word *love* in the presence of David.

She broke free of his fingers and his searching gaze, darted down the steps and across the back lawn.

"Kayla," he called. "Stop."

But she didn't. Stop why? So that he could dissect her heartbreak? Lay open her disappointments with his eyes? No, she kept on going. Nothing could stop her.

Except his next words.

"Kayla, stop. I think I see the dog."

CHAPTER EIGHT

AT FIRST KAYLA THOUGHT it was a trick. Kevin had not been above using what she wanted most to get his own way.

Once we get established, in our new town, then we can talk about a baby.

She whirled, already angry that something about David being here was bringing all this *stuff* up. She was prepared to be very angry if David had used her dog to make her do what he wanted.

He was not looking at her, but had gone to the railing of his deck and was watching something intently. She followed David' gaze, and though it was dark, she saw Bastigal's little rump, tail tucked hard between his legs, disappearing through the Blazes' hedges and heading out onto the street.

Kayla's heart leaped with hope.

David stepped back inside the door, shoved his feet in a pair of sneakers and went down the back porch steps two at a time. He blasted through the boxwood, careless of the branches scraping him.

Kayla looked down at her own bare feet, and contemplated the skimpy fabric of her night-gown. By the time she went and got shoes on, or grabbed a sweater to cover herself—her sweater had gone inside with Mrs. Blaze—the dog would be gone. She doubted Bastigal would come to David even if he did manage to catch up to him.

It was the middle of the night. It was not as if anyone was going to see her.

Except him. David. And he thought I should be painted.

Without nearly enough thought, with a spontaneity that felt wonderfully freeing, Kayla took off through the hedge after David.

She saw he was crossing the deserted street at a dead run. If Kayla had had any doubt that he had maintained the athleticism of a decade before, it was vanquished. He ran like the wind, effortless, his strides long and ground covering. In the blink of an eye, David had crossed the silvered front lawn of a house across the street. Without breaking stride he charged around the side of a house and disappeared into the back-yard.

She followed him. She thought her feet would

give her grief, but in actual fact she had spent all the summers of her life barefoot, and she loved the feeling of the grass on them, velvety, dewy, perfect lawns springing beneath her feet.

She arrived in the backyard just in time to watch David hurdle effortlessly over a low picket fence into the next yard. She scrambled over it, catching her nightie. She yanked it free and kept running. She didn't see Bastigal, but David must have seen the dog, because he was chasing after something like a hound on the scent.

She caught up with David after finding her way through a set of particularly prickly hedges. They were in the middle of someone's back lawn. She cast a glance at the darkened windows.

"Do you see him?" she whispered.

He held a finger to his lips, and they both listened, and heard a rustle in the thick shrubs that bordered the lawn.

"Bastigal!" Kayla called in a stage whisper, both not wanting to frighten the dog or wake the neighbors.

Twigs cracked and leaves rustled, but she didn't catch so much as a glimpse of her dog, and the sound was moving determinedly away from them.

David moved cautiously toward it. She tiptoed after him. And then David was off like a sprinter out of the blocks, and Kayla kept on his heels.

Three blocks later, she had done the fast tour of every backyard in the neighborhood, and they now found themselves on Peachtree Lane, in the front yard of a house that was on Blossom Valley's register of most notable heritage homes.

"I think we lost him," David said, and put his hands on his knees, bent forward at the waist and tried to catch his breath.

"Dammit." She followed his lead and rested her hands on her knees, bent over and gasping for air. She was so close to him she could see the shine of perspiration on his brow, the tangy, sweet scent of a clean man's sweat tickled her nostrils.

"Don't move a muscle," David whispered. He nodded toward the deep shadow of a shrub drooping under the weight of heavy purple blossoms.

One of the blossoms stirred in the windless night. The leaves parted.

Kayla stopped gasping and held her breath.

A little beige-colored bunny came out, blinked its pinky eyes at them and wiggled its nose.

"Is that what we've been chasing?" she asked.

"I think so."

"Dammit," she said for the second time.

But despite her disappointment, Kayla was aware that her blood felt as if it were humming through her veins, and that she felt wonderfully, delightfully alive.

She began to laugh. She tried to muffle her laughter so as not to disturb the sleeping neighborhood.

David straightened, watched her, arms folded over his chest. He shook his head, and then smiled. Then he chuckled.

She collapsed on the grass, on her back, knees up. She tugged her nightie, now torn at the hem where it had snagged, down over her bare knees, and then spread her arms wide, giggling and still panting, trying to catch her breath.

After a moment, David flopped down on his back beside her, his arm thrown up over his forehead.

Their breathing became less ragged, and the night seemed deeply silent. Some delicious fragrance tickled her nostrils. The stars were magnificent in an inky black sky.

"This is one of the things I missed after we moved to Windsor," Kayla whispered. "You don't see the stars like this in the city."

"No," he agreed softly, "you don't."

The silence was deep and companionable between them. "Why did you move to Windsor?" he asked. "You always liked it here."

I hoped for a fresh start. I hoped a baby could repair some of the things we had lost.

Out loud, she said, "Kevin got a job there."

She didn't say that Kevin's job had not lasted, but by then they could not afford to move back, let alone have a baby. She did not say the kind of jobs she had done to keep them afloat. She had waitressed and cleaned and babysat children and even done yard work.

She did not say how she had longed for the sweetness of the life she had left behind in her hometown. Didn't David long for it like that? She asked him.

"Do you miss it here? Ever?"

His silence was long. "No, Kayla. I don't have time to miss it."

"If you did have time, would you?"

Again the silence was long. And then, almost reluctantly, he said, "Yeah, I guess I would. Blossom Valley was the place of perfect summers, wasn't it?"

The longing was poignant between them.

"I can't remember the last time I looked at the stars like this," she murmured. But she thought it was probably in those carefree days, those days before everything had changed.

"Me, either."

It was one of those absolutely spontaneous perfect moments. His bare shoulder was nearly touching hers. Peripherally, she was aware of the rise and fall of his naked chest, and that it was his scent, mingled with the pure scent of the dew on the grass and the night air and those flowers drooping under their own weight, that had made the night so deliciously fragrant.

"Is that Orion above us?" he asked.

"Yes," she said, "the hunter."

"I remembered how you impressed me once by naming all the stars in that constellation."

She laughed softly. "Zeta, Epsilon, Delta. That's his belt."

"Go on."

So she did, naming the stars of the constellation, one by one, and then they lay in silence, contemplating the night sky above them.

"I always thought you'd become a teacher," he said slowly. "You had such an amazing mind, took such delight in learning things."

She said nothing, another road not taken rising up before her.

"I at least thought you'd have kids. You always loved kids. You were always a counselor at that awful day camp. What was it called?"

"Sparkling Waters. And it wasn't awful. It was for kids who couldn't afford camp."

"Naturally," he said drily. "One of the most affluent communities in Canada, and you find the needy kids. I didn't even know there were any until you started working there."

"That whole neighborhood south of the tracks is full of orchard workers and people who clean rooms at the motels and hotels." She didn't tell him that now that she had been one of those people she had even more of an affinity for them. "It was Blossom Valley's dirty little secret then, and it still is today."

"And how are you going to fix that?" he asked.

Instead of feeling annoyed, she felt oddly safe with him. She replied, "I bet I could think of some kind of coupon system so the kids can come for ice cream."

"Ah, Kayla," he said, but not with recrimination.

"That's me. Changing the world, one ice cream cone at a time."

"No wonder those kids adored you," he remembered wryly. "What I remember is if we saw the kids you worked with during the day at night, they wanted to hang out with you. I hated that. Us ultracool teenagers with all these little tagalongs."

"Maybe you were ultracool. I wasn't."

"I probably wasn't, either," he said, that wryness still in his voice. "But I sure thought I was. Maybe all guys that age think they are."

Certainly Kevin had thought he was, too, Kayla remembered. But he never really had been. Funny, yes. Charming, absolutely. Good-looking, but not spectacularly so. Athletic, but never a star. Energetic and mischievous and fun-loving.

Kevin had always been faintly and subtly competitive with his better-looking and stronger best friend.

When David signed up for lifeguard training, so did Kevin, but he didn't just want to be equal to David, he wanted to be better. So if David swam across the lake, Kevin swam there and back. When David bought his first car—that rusting little foreign import—Kevin, make that Kevin's father, bought a brand-new one.

The faint edge to Kevin's relationship with David seemed like something everyone but David had been aware of.

Hadn't Kayla spent much of her marriage trying to convince Kevin he was good enough? Trying to convince him that she was not in the least bowled over by David's many successes that were making all the newspapers? Trying to forgive Kevin's jealousy and bitterness toward his friend, excuse it as *caused* by

David's indifference to the man who had once been his friend?

But Kayla remembered David *really* had been ultracool. Even back then he'd had something—a presence, an intensity, a way of taking charge—that had set him apart.

And made him irresistible to almost every girl in town. *And on one magic night, I'd been the girl. That he had shared his remarkable charisma with.*

I tasted his lips, and then he hardly looked at me again.

"I adored them back," she said, wanting to remember the affection of those moments and not the sense of loss his sudden indifference had caused in her.

"They were pesky little rascals," David said. "You never told them to go away and leave you—us—alone. I can remember you passing out hot dogs—that I had provided—to them at a campfire."

Maybe that was why he had stopped speaking to me.

"Did I?"

"Yeah. And marshmallows. Our soda pop. Nothing was safe."

"I love kids," she said softly. "I probably couldn't bear to think of them hungry."

"Our little do-gooder." He paused and looked

at her. "You did love kids, though. That's why I thought you'd lose no time having a pile of them of your own. Especially since you seemed in such a hurry to get married."

Kayla bit her lip. For the first time since they had lain down beneath the stars, she was certain she heard judgment there.

Marry in haste, repent at leisure.

"So why didn't you have kids?" he persisted.

Kayla begged herself not to even think it. But the soft night air, and this unexpected moment, lying in the coolness of the grass beside David, made the thought explode inside of her.

She had wanted a child, desperately. Now she could see it was a blessing she had not had one.

"The time was just never right," she said, her tone cool, not inviting any more questions.

"Aw, Kayla," he said, and as unforthcoming as she thought her statement had been, she felt as if David heard every unhappy moment of her marriage in it.

She felt an abrupt, defensive need to take the focus off herself. "So why aren't you married, David? Why don't you have a wife and kids and a big, happy family?"

"At first it was because I never met anyone I wanted to do those things with," he said quietly.

"Come on. You've become news with some

of the women you dated! Kelly O'Ranahan? Beautiful, successful, talented."

"Insecure, superficial, wouldn't know Orion if he shot her with an arrow."

The moment suddenly seemed shot through with more than an arrow. Heat sizzled between them as his gaze locked on hers.

"What do you mean, 'at first'?" she whispered.

He didn't answer—he just reached out and slid a hand through her hair, and looked at her with such longing it stole her breath from her lungs.

The air felt ripe with possibilities. Kayla again felt seen, somehow, in a way no one had seen her for years.

Somehow, feeling that way made her feel more intensely guilty than her disloyal thoughts about her husband.

And then, thankfully, the uncomfortable intensity of the moment was shattered when the darkness exploded around them, and they were both frozen in an orb of white light.

"End to a perfect day," she said, happy for the distraction from the intensity. "Beesting, hospital emergency room, lost dog—" *disloyal thoughts about my deceased husband* "—now alien kidnapping."

He didn't smile at her attempt to use humor to deflect the intensity between them.

"Don't forget the stargazing part," he said softly.

She looked at him. Not many people would look better under the harsh glare of the light that illuminated them, but he did. It brought the strength of his features into sharp relief.

It occurred to her that the stargazing was the part she was least likely to forget.

David broke the gaze first, sat up and shielded his eyes against the bright light that held them.

"Police! Get up off that grass."

CHAPTER NINE

THEIR PREDICAMENT STRUCK KAYLA as hilarious, but she suspected her sudden desire to laugh was like biting back laughter at a funeral. Her nerves were strung tight over the moments they had just shared. Her emotions felt electric, overwhelming and way too close to the surface.

Could David possibly think she was more attractive than Kelly O'Ranahan, the famous actress?

Of course not! She was reading way too much into his hand finding her hair and touching it. He probably felt nothing but sorry for her.

"Put your hands in the air where I can see them."

Poor David. She cast a look at his face. If David had been ultracool back then, he was even more so now. A proven track record of ultracoolness.

It occurred to her she was about to get one

of Canada's most respected businessmen arrested. It was no laughing matter, really, but she couldn't help herself.

She laughed.

David shot her a look that warned her he wasn't finding it in any way as amusing as she was. His expression was grim as he reached for her hand and found it. Then he got his feet underneath him and jumped up lithely, yanking her up beside him.

She noticed he stepped out just a little in front of her, shielding her torn nightie-clad body from the harshness of the police searchlight with his own.

It reminded her of something a long time ago—a thunderstorm, and seeking shelter under the awning of the ice cream store. She remembered him pulling off his shirt and putting it over her own, which had become transparent with wetness.

Was it in some way weak—a further betrayal of her marriage—to enjoy his protective instincts so much? He let go of her hand only after he had put her behind him, and then shaded his eyes, trying to see past the light.

"Sir, I need you to put your hands up in the air. You, too, ma'am."

The light they were caught in was absolutely blinding. Kayla squinted past the broadness of

David's shoulder and into the brightness. She could make out the dark outline of Blossom Valley's only patrol car.

She did as asked, but the laughter had started deep inside her and she had to choke it back. She slid a look at David. His expression was grim as he put his hands up, rested them with laced fingers on the top of his head.

The spotlight went off, and a policeman came across the lawn toward them. He looked grumpy as he stopped a few feet away and regarded them with deep suspicion. He took a notepad from his pocket, licked his pencil, waiting.

When neither of them volunteered anything, he said, "We've had a report of a prowler in this area."

Kayla bit her lip to try and stop the giggle, but she made the mistake of casting a glance at David's face. Naturally, he was appalled by their predicament, his face cast in stone. A snort of laughter escaped her.

"Have you folks been drinking?"

"No," David bit out, giving her a withering glance when another snort of laughter escaped her.

"I'm sorry," she managed to sputter.

"Is this your house?"

"No," David snapped.

"Have you got any ID?"

"Does it look like we have any ID?" David said, exasperated and losing patience fast. She cast him a glance, and saw instantly that he was not intimidated, that he was a man who was very accustomed to being in authority, not knuckling under to it.

"Well, what are you doing half-dressed in front of a house that isn't yours? How do you know each other?"

David sucked in a harsh breath at the insinuation that they might have been doing something improper. He took a step forward, but Kayla stepped out of his protection and inserted herself, hands still on top of her head, between him and the policeman. She sensed David's irritation with her.

"We're neighbors. We're looking for my dog," Kayla said hastily, before David really did manage to get himself arrested. "We thought we saw him and gave chase. I'm afraid we did trespass through several backyards. It turned out to be that bunny over there."

"What bunny?"

Kayla turned and lowered one arm to point, but the bunny, naturally, had disappeared. "There really was one. We haven't been drinking." She could feel a blush moving up her cheeks as she realized a nightie that was perfectly respectable in her house was not so much on the darkened streets of Blossom Valley.

"Or doing anything else," she said, lowering her other arm and folding both of them over the sheerness of her nightie.

The policeman regarded them both, then his suspicion died and he sighed.

"You can put your hands down. My little girl has been looking for that dog since the posters went up. She went to sleep dreaming about the reward. She wants a new bicycle." He squinted at David. "Do I know you?"

David lowered his arms and lifted an eyebrow in a way that said *I doubt it*. How could he manage to have such presence, even in such an awkward situation?

"Are you that investor guy?" the cop asked. Deference, similar to that Kayla had heard in the care aide's voice, crept into the policeman's tone. "The one I saw the article about in *Lakeside Life?*"

"That would be me."

"You don't look much like a prowler, actually."

"Do most prowlers not go out and about in their pajamas?" David asked a bit drily.

"Well, not Slugs and Snails pajamas," the officer said, recognizing the name brand of a Canadian clothing icon that produced very sought after—and very, very expensive—men's casual clothing.

Kayla squinted at David's pajama bottoms. They did, indeed, have the very subtle label of the men's designer firm, and she had to admire the officer's professional powers of observation.

She also had to bite back another giggle as she realized her own attire, her summer-weight, white nightie, might be worthy of a painting, but it was way too revealing. She maneuvered back into the shadow cast by David.

David shot her a warning look over his shoulder when she had to bite back another giggle.

"What do you think of AIM?" the policeman asked, putting the dark writing pad he'd held in his hand back into his shirt pocket. He snapped a flashlight onto his belt.

"Personally, I think it's a dog," David said.

"Unfortunately, not the dog we are looking for," Kayla inserted helpfully.

David gave her a look over his shoulder, and then continued as if she hadn't spoken, "If you have it, now's the time to dump it. If you don't have it, don't buy it. Try—" he smiled a bit "—Slugs and Snails. It trades as SAS-B.TO."

"Really?"

David lifted a shoulder. "If you're into taking advice from a half-naked man in his pajamas in the middle of the night."

The policeman finally relaxed completely. Now it was all buddy to buddy. He laughed. "Well, the pajamas are Slugs and Snails. How far are you from home?"

"Sugar Maple," David said.

"I can give you a lift back over there."

"No!" David's answer was instant. "Thanks anyway."

"Speak for yourself," Kayla said firmly. "It's a perfect finish for this day—a ride in the backseat of a police car. Plus, it's on my bucket list."

David glared at her. "Why would that be on your bucket list?"

"Because it's what everyone least expects of me."

"You got that right," David growled.

But a deeper part of the truth was that Kayla knew David wouldn't get in the police car because he would be aware, as she was, that everyone had phones and cameras these days. He was the CEO of a company that relied on his reputation being squeaky clean. He was publically recognizable because of his success and his involvement with well-known and high-profile people. Kelly O'Ranahan was only one of a long list.

David Blaze was a public figure. Kayla

didn't really blame him for not getting in, but she was aware as she smiled at him, as the policeman opened the door for her and she slid into the backseat, that she needed for this encounter with David to be over.

She felt she had, somehow, revealed too much of herself on the basis of a starry night and an old friendship.

Now she felt the vulnerability of her confessions, felt faintly ashamed of herself and as if she had betrayed Kevin.

But worse than any of that? The yearning she had felt when David had reached out and touched her hair.

Kayla felt she had to escape him.

Being determined that he would not see any of that, she gave David a cheeky wave as she drove away in the police car.

And then she let the relief well up in her, a feeling as if she was escaping something dangerous and unpredictable and uncontrollable.

She liked being in control. Especially after Kevin.

"Hey, good luck with your dog," the cop said, a few minutes later. He very sweetly got out and opened the car door for her before he drove away.

Despite the fact her day had unfolded as a series of mishaps, and her dog was missing, and she had discovered, within herself, an unspoken bitterness toward Kevin, Kayla was uncomfortably aware of something as she climbed the dilapidated stairs to her house.

She felt alive. She felt intensely and vibrantly alive, possibly for the first time since she had left Blossom Valley.

She could not even remember the last time she had laughed so hard as when the police light had been turned on her and David.

Her life, she realized, had been way too serious for way too long. When had she lost her ability to be spontaneous?

But she already knew. Her marriage had become an ongoing effort to control everything—fun had become a distant memory.

Yearning grabbed her again. To feel alive. To laugh.

Despite the hour, Kayla didn't feel like sleeping. She didn't feel ready, somehow, to leave the night—with its odd combination of magic and self-discovery and discomfort—behind. She went into the kitchen, turned on the light, opened the fridge.

Somehow, drinking lemonade on her front porch and watching the sun come up sounded wonderful in a way it would not have even a day ago.

And who knew? Maybe she would even see

Bastigal wandering home from his own adventure.

But it was the thought that maybe she was really waiting to see David again that made her rethink it. She closed the fridge door—and the door on all her secret longings. She turned off the lights and ordered herself to bed.

But not before having one last peek out the window. She told herself she was having one last look for Bastigal, and yet her stomach did a funny downward swoop when she watched David come down the street.

Kayla sank back in the shadows of her house as she watched David take the front steps of the house next door. He pulled up the screen and tried the handle.

Kayla realized the care aide had decided to do her job *now*. The front door was locked up tight.

Telling herself it was none of her business, she went to a side window and watched him go to the back door of his house. It was the same. Locked.

He tried a window. Locked. Kayla noticed all the windows were closed, which was a real shame on such a beautiful night—but she realized all sorts of precautions would be in place to try and ensure his mother's well-being.

As she continued to watch, David went back

to the door and knocked lightly. Kayla could tell he did not want to wake his mother if she was sleeping. Presumably the care aide was not, but she did not come to the door, either. Watching television, maybe?

He stepped back off the steps, and Kayla could tell he was contemplating his options.

She could offer him her couch, of course. He had rescued her today—no, given the lateness of the hour, that was yesterday already—after she'd been stung.

She'd only be returning the favor.

But she remembered his deeply sarcastic tone when he had said earlier today: *Kayla to the rescue.*

And then, a certain wryness in his tone, he had remembered her working at that camp, those children trailing her through town.

Really, more of the same.

Kayla to the rescue. It made her aware that she *needed* to resist whatever was going on in her.

She was going to go to bed, and she was going to mind her own business and not feel the least bit guilty about it, either.

Not even when she peeked back out her window and saw him dragging a thick cushion off the patio furniture down the deck steps and onto the lush grass of his mother's backyard.

She watched him lay it out a few feet from the bottom of the steps, and then lie down on top of it, on his back, his face toward the sky as if he could not get enough of the stars tonight. Some tension left him, and she was not sure she had ever seen a person look more relaxed.

And she envied him for the place he had among the stars. Had she offered her couch and had he taken it, she would have deprived him of this moment.

It occurred to her that maybe that's what rescuing did: gave the rescuer a feeling of power while keeping the rescued person from their own destiny, from finding their own way to where they were supposed to be.

And in light of her relationship with Kevin, that was a deeply distressing thought.

Kayla decided, right then and there, that she was going to avoid David for the rest of the time he spent here with his mother.

She did not need the kind of introspection he seemed to be triggering in her. And she certainly did not need the complication of a man who could cause her to ache with yearning just by touching her hair!

CHAPTER TEN

DAVID CONTEMPLATED THE STARS above his head. He could sleep in his car, except he had put the roof up at dark and locked it. His keys were inside the house. Ditto for his wallet, or he could go get a hotel room somewhere, though of course hotels would be booked solid at this time of year in Blossom Valley.

If his mother managed to get out the back door again, he had her escape route, and the route to the garden shed, blocked.

What do you mean "at first"? Kayla had asked him about his choice not to marry, not to have children.

At first it had been because he had never found the right person. Now it went so much deeper. Some forms of his mother's illness had a genetic component. What if he had it?

And his father had died young of heart disease, plunging the family he had protected so diligently into a despair deeper than the ocean.

David's doctor had assured him his own heart was the heart of an athlete. And the other? There was a test they could do to determine the presence of the "E" gene.

But so far, David had said no. Did you want to know something like that? Why would you? Just for yourself, no. If there was someone else involved in his life...?

Was it the strangely delightful evening with Kayla making him have these wayward thoughts?

He decided firmly, and not for the first time, that he was not going there, that these kind of thoughts were counterproductive. They had snuck by his defenses only because he was exhausted. He closed his eyes, drew in one long breath and ordered himself to sleep. And it worked.

David woke up feeling amazingly refreshed. The sun was already warm on his face, and he glanced at his watch, astounded by how late he had slept and how well. He realized he was glad to have slept outside.

The inside was not really a house anymore: doors locked, cleaning supplies hidden, windows never opened, stove unplugged. One of the live-in care aides had moved into his boyhood bedroom, and he was relegated to a tiny den with a pullout sofa when he came.

David got up swiftly, not wanting to dwell on all the depressing issues inside his mother's house. He returned the cushions to the deck that was never used anymore, except by that care aide he suspected of slipping outside to sneak cigarettes.

What had he said last night to Kayla? That his mother's house looked like normal people lived here. He was aware, the feeling of being refreshed leaving him, that he had probably kept that particular illusion alive too long.

It wasn't safe for his mother to be here anymore.

He would look at options for her today. He was aware of feeling that there was no time to lose.

He would look after it and leave here. For good, this time.

David knocked on the door, and this time it was opened by a new aide, who must have arrived to help the live-in with morning chores. She looked at him with an expression as bewildered as his mother's.

"It's a long story," he said and moved by the aide.

His mother was in the kitchen, toying with her breakfast, an unappetizing-looking lump of porridge that had been cooked in the microwave. At one time David had hired a cook, but his mother had become so querulous and suspicious of everyone that staff did not stay no matter what he offered to pay them. Then there had been the issue of her sneaking down in the night and turning on the stove burners.

But this morning his mother was dressed, and everything matched and was done up correctly and her hair was combed so he knew she'd had help. The thorn scratches on her arms had been freshly treated with ointment but were a reminder of what he needed to do.

He left the house as soon as he had showered and put on a fresh shirt and shorts from a suitcase he did not bother to unpack. He went downtown and had breakfast. His mother, obviously, had no internet, and for many years he hadn't stayed long enough to miss it. Now, after a frustrating phone call, he found out it would take weeks to get it hooked up.

He drove down to the beach, still quiet in the morning, and began to make phone calls.

The first was to his assistant, Jane, a middle-aged girl Friday worth her weight in gold.

With her he caught up on some business transactions and gave instructions for putting out a few minor fires. Then, aware of feeling a deep sadness, he told Jane what he needed her to research. A care home, probably private, that specialized in people with dementia.

"See if you can send me some virtual tours," he said, stripping the emotion from his own voice when she sounded concerned. Then, as an afterthought, maybe to try and banish what he was setting in motion, he said, "And see what you can find out about an ice cream parlor for sale here in Blossom Valley. It's called More-moo."

He was aware, as he put away his phone, that his heart was beating too fast, and not from asking his assistant to find out about the ice cream parlor.

From betraying his mother's trust.

Not that she trusted me, he reminded himself, attempting wryness. But it fell flat inside his own heart and left the most enormous feeling of pain he'd ever felt.

Unless you counted the time he'd witnessed Kayla say *I do* to the wrong man.

"I hate coming home," he muttered to himself. He stepped out of the car and gazed out at the familiar water.

And suddenly he didn't hate coming home quite so much. The water. It had always been his solace.

After a moment he locked the phone in the car and went down to the beach. He took off his shirt and left it in the sand. The shorts would dry quickly enough. He dove into the cool, clear water of the bay and struck out across it.

An hour and a half later he crawled from the water, exhausted and so cold he was numb. And yet, still, he could not bring himself to go home.

No point without a Wi-Fi connection, anyway, he told himself. He drove downtown, bought some dry shorts and looked for a restaurant that offered internet.

It happened to be More-moo, and David decided he could check out some of the more obvious parts of their operation himself.

He managed to conduct business from there for most of the day. Jane sent him several links to places with euphemistic names like Shady Oak and Sunset Court, which he could not bring himself to open. She sent him the financials for More-moo, which he felt guilty looking at, with that sweet grandmotherly type telling him, *No, no, you're no bother at all, honey.* And keeping his coffee cup filled to the brim.

Whatever reason they were selling, it wasn't their service, their cleanliness or their coffee. All three were excellent.

He brought dinner home for his mother, rather than face the smells of some kind of liver and broccoli puree coming out of the microwave.

She had no idea who he was.

That night, it seemed so easy just to go and drag the cushions back off the deck furniture and lie again, under the stars, protecting the back exit from his mother's escape.

He was aware of a light going on in Kayla's house, and then of it going off again. He both wanted to go see her and wanted to avoid her.

He hadn't had a single call about the dog, but he was pretty sure it wasn't his failure keeping him away.

It felt like the compassion in her eyes could break him wide open.

And if that happened? How would he put himself back together again? How?

Tomorrow he was going to force himself to look at some of the websites for care homes. Tomorrow he was going to force himself to call some of the numbers Jane had supplied him with.

Tonight he was going to sleep under the stars, and somehow wish that he were over-reacting. That when he went in the house tomorrow he would see his mother was better, and that it was not necessary to make a decision at all.

But in the morning, after he'd showered and

shaved and dressed, he went into a kitchen that smelled sour, and his mother had *that* look on her face.

She looked up from her bowl of porridge—surely at Shady Oak they would manage something more appetizing—and glared at him.

David braced himself. She held up a sweater she'd been holding on her lap, stroking it as though it were a cat.

"Where did this come from, young man?"

"I'm sure it's yours, Mom."

"It's not!" she said triumphantly. "It belongs to Kayla McIntosh."

He tried not to look too surprised that she remembered Kayla's name. It had been a long time since she had remembered his. Even if it was Kayla's maiden name, it made him wonder if he was being too hasty. Maybe no decisions had to be made today.

"You go give it back to her. Right now! I won't have your ill-gotten gains in this house, young man."

He took the sweater. Of course he didn't have to go give it to Kayla—it probably wasn't even hers. But he caught a faint scent overriding the terrible scents that had become the reality of his mother's home.

The sweater smelled of freshness and lemons, and he realized Kayla must have given it to his mother the other night when she had found her in the roses.

Was it the scent of Kayla that made him not pay enough attention? Or was it just that a man couldn't be on red alert around his own mother all the time?

The porridge bowl whistled by his ear and crashed against the wall behind him. All the dishes were plastic now, but the porridge dripped down the wall.

"Mrs. Blaze!" the attendant said, aghast. The look she shot David was loaded with unwanted sympathy.

He cleared his throat against the lump that had risen in it, that felt as if it was going to choke him.

He said to the caregiver, his voice level, "When I was a little boy, my mother took the garden hose and flooded the backyard in the winter so I could skate. She made lemonade for my stand, and helped me with the sign, and didn't say a word that I sold five bucks worth of lemonade for two dollars. She never missed a single swim meet when I was on the swim team, and they must have numbered in the hundreds.

"She stayed up all night and held me the night my father died, worried about my grief when her own must have been unbearable. She lent me the money to buy my first car, even though she had been putting away a little bit of money every week trying to get a new stove.

"My mother was the most amazing person you could ever meet. She was funny and kind and smart. At the same time, she was dignified and courageous.

"I need you to know that," he said quietly. "I need you to think about what she once was. I need that to be as important to you as what she is now."

"Yes, sir," the aide said.

"I remember the skating rink," his mother whispered. "My mittens got wet and my hands were so cold I couldn't feel them. The bottom of my pants froze, like trying to walk in stove-pipes. But I wouldn't stop. Wanted to surprise him. The ice froze funny, all lumpy. But he was out there, every night, skating. My boy. My boy."

David had to squeeze the bridge of his nose, hard.

"I'll return the sweater right now," he said, as if nothing had happened. He went out the door, gulping in air like a man who had escaped a smoke-filled building. He heard the locks click in place behind him.

He drew in a long breath, contemplating his options, again. He tucked the sweater under his arm and went out his gate. He paused in that familiar stretch of lawn between the two houses.

As much as he logically knew the illness was making terrifying inroads on her mind, it hurt that his mother saw him as a thief and untrustworthy, that she could remember Kayla's name, but not his. It hurt that she had become a person who would throw her breakfast at anyone, let alone at her son.

But she remembered the skating rink, and so did he, and the pain he felt almost made him sorry he had brought it up.

He thought, *This is why, now, I will not get married and have children. I cannot do this to another person. I cannot pass this on to another person.*

Was he thinking these kind of thoughts because Kayla, at some level, was making him long for things he was aware he could not have?

Drawing in a deep breath, David went through Kayla's back gate. He would hang the sweater on her back door, then walk to the lake and swim. He was developing a routine of sorts, and he loved the cold water in the morning, when the beach was still deserted.

He went up the stairs to Kayla's back deck and eyed the patio furniture—four old Adirondack chairs, grouped together. Once, he seemed to remember, they had been light blue, but now the wood was gray and weathered. The chairs looked like they would offer slivers rather than comfort. The deck was in about the same condition as the chairs. It had not been stained in so long that the exposed wood had rotted and was probably past repair.

He went to hang the sweater on the back door handle. He noticed only the screen door was closed, the storm door open behind it, leaving a clear view into the cheeriness of the kitchen.

Was that safe? Even in Blossom Valley?

He had just decided it was none of his business when Kayla came to the door. She didn't have a scrap of makeup on and had her honey-colored hair scraped back in a ponytail. She was wearing a bib apron tied over a too-large T-shirt and faded denim shorts.

The contrast to his world of super sophistication—women who wore designer duds even when they were dressed casually, and who were never seen in public without makeup on and hair done—was both jarring and refreshing.

Kayla looked *real*. She also looked as if she had been up for hours, and the smell of toast—so normal it hurt his heart—wafted out the door.

For a moment she looked disconcerted to see him—not nearly as pleased to be caught

in such a natural state as he had been to catch
her in it—but then her expression brightened.

"Have you heard something about Bastigal?"
she asked eagerly.

"No, I'm sorry. I just brought you back your
sweater."

"Oh." She looked crushed. "Thanks."

She opened the door, and it screeched out-
rageously on rusting hinges. He noticed she
didn't even have the hook latched on it.

"Do you have a phone yet?" he asked.

"Not yet."

"You should get one," he said, "and you
should lock your door. At least do up the latch
on the screen."

She looked annoyed at his concern, rather
than grateful. "This is Blossom Valley," she
said. "You and I 'prowling' was probably the
biggest news on the criminal front in years."

"Bad stuff happens everywhere," he said
sternly.

"If it's safe enough for you to sleep out under
the stars, it's safe enough for me to leave my
screen door unlatched."

He glared at her.

"The latch is broken," she said with a re-
signed sigh. "The wood around it is rotted."

"Oh."

She bristled under what she interpreted as

sympathy or judgment or both. "And how are you sleeping in the great outdoors? Fending off mosquitoes?"

Did she mutter a barely audible "I hope"?

Was he trying to control the locks on Kayla's doors because his own world seemed so unsafe and unpredictable—beyond saving—at least where his mother was concerned?

Several retorts played on his tongue, *never better, reminds me of my boy scout days*—but it shocked him when the truth spilled out.

"I hate it in that house," David said, his voice quiet. "I hate how the way it is now feels like it could steal the way it once was completely from my mind. Steal Christmas mornings, and the night I graduated from high school and the way my mom looked when my dad pinned that rose corsage on her for their fifteenth anniversary, right before he died. The way that house is now could steal the moment the puppy came home, and the memories of the dog he grew to be."

He blinked hard, amazed the words had come out past the lump that had been in his throat since his mother had thrown her porridge at him, but then remembered the backyard skating rink.

David was both annoyed with himself and relieved to have spoken it.

Kayla's bristling over her unlocked door, and her glee at his sleeping arrangements, melted. "Oh, David, I'm so sorry."

He ordered himself to walk away, to follow his original plan to go to the lake and let the ice-cold water and the physical exertion take it all.

Instead, when the door squeaked open and Kayla stepped back, inviting him into her house, he found himself moving by her as if he had no choice at all.

He entered her kitchen like a man who had crossed the desert and known thirst and hardship, and who had found an oasis that promised cool protection from the harshness of the sun, and that promised a long, cold drink of water.

He looked around her kitchen. He had spent a lot of his growing-up years in this room and this room was as unchanged as his own house was changed.

A large French-paned window faced the backyard. It was already a bright room, but Mrs. Jaffrey had painted the walls sunshine-yellow, and though the yellow had faded, the effect was still one of cheer.

The cabinets were old and had seen better days, and nobody had that kind of countertop anymore. The table had been painted dozens of times and every one of the color choices showed through the blemishes in the paint. It was leaning unsteadily, one of the legs shorter than the others. The appliances were old porcelain models, black showing through the chipped white enamel.

The kitchen was unchanged, but still he felt something catch in his throat. Because although the room was the same, wasn't this just more of the same of what was going on next door?

He could practically see Kevin sitting at that table, gulping down milk and gobbling down still-warm cookies, leaving dribbles of chocolate on his lips.

He could see Kevin's devil-may-care smile, almost hear his shout of laughter.

David realized he had lied to Kayla when she had asked him why he had never chosen marriage and a family.

And when she had asked him if he ever missed *this,* for this kitchen was really the heart and soul of what growing up in Blossom Valley had been.

Right now, particularly vulnerable because of what had just happened with his mother, he missed how everything used to be so much that he felt like he could lay his head on that table and cry like a wounded animal.

Kevin was dead, but even before his death,

had been the death of their friendship, which had been just as painful. Now, the Jaffreys had moved. It seemed shocking that Kayla was Mrs. Jaffrey now.

Really, with the death of his father, David felt as if he had begun to learn a lesson that had not really stopped since: love was leaving yourself open to a series of breathtaking losses.

And still, this kitchen softened something in him that did not want to be softened.

The kitchen was a mess of the nicest kind: recipe books open, mixing bowls out, blobs of yellowy batter—lemon chiffon cake, at this time of the day?—spattering the counter. David was painfully aware that there was a feeling of homecoming here that he no longer had at home.

He realized some of it was scent: Kayla's scent, lemony and sweet, that clung to her, and the sweater he was holding. There was the fresh smell of the toast she'd had for breakfast, but underneath that he remembered more good things. He swore he could smell all the cookies that had ever been baked in that archaic oven, and Thanksgiving dinner, and golden-crusted pies that lined the countertops after the original Mrs. Jaffrey had availed herself of Blossom Valley's apple harvest.

He compared that to the hospital smells of

his mother's house—disinfectants and unappetizing food heated in the microwave and smells he did not even want to think about—and he felt like he never wanted to leave this kitchen again.

"Mom asked me to return your sweater," he said past the lump in his throat. "She remembered your name."

Kayla scanned his face and took the sweater wordlessly from his hands, hanging it on the back of one of the chairs.

There. He'd done what he came to do. He needed to be in the water, to swim until his muscles hurt and until his mind could not think a single thought. Instead, he found himself reluctant to leave this kitchen that said home to him in a way his mother's home would never do again.

Instead, he found himself wishing Kayla would press her hand over his heart again.

"Are you okay?" she asked him.

No. "Yes."

But she seemed to hear the *no* as if he had spoken it.

She regarded him thoughtfully. It was as if she could see every sorrow that he carried within him.

"I'm trying out recipes in an effort to keep

busy and keep my mind off Bastigal. Would you like to try some homemade ice cream?"

He thought of the congealed porridge at his house. He thought he had to say no to this. He was in a weakened state. This could not go anywhere good.

But suddenly none of that mattered. He had carried his burdens in solitude for so long and it felt, ridiculously, as if they could be eased by this kitchen, by her, by the appeal of home-made ice cream.

He could not have said no to her invitation if he wanted to.

CHAPTER ELEVEN

To admit Kayla's kitchen, and her invitation, and Kayla herself, were proving impossible to say no to felt as if it would be some kind of defeat, so instead of saying yes, David just lifted a shoulder as if he could care less whether he ate her ice cream or not.

Kayla did not seem to be fooled, and her eyes were gentle as they lingered on his face. Then she acted just as if she had heard the *yes* that he had not spoken.

"It's not quite ready. Give me a second."

"I hope it's not rose petal," he said, needing her to know he had not surrendered to her charms or the charms of her kitchen completely.

"Oh, way better than that."

"But what could be?" he said drily.

"I bought this at a yard sale," she said, turning away from him and back to her crowded countertop. She lifted off her counter a bowl big enough to bathe a baby in.

At first he thought she meant she had purchased the bowl at a yard sale but then she trundled over to a stainless-steel apparatus that squatted on her floor with a certain inexplicable air of malevolence. He wasn't sure how he hadn't noticed it before since it took up a whole corner of the kitchen.

"What is it?" he asked warily, and gratefully, as something in him shifted away from that awful picture of porridge dripping down the wall in his house next door.

"It's called a batch freezer!" Kayla said triumphantly. "What are the chances I would find one just as I'm contemplating buying an ice cream store?"

"Cosmically ordained," he said.

She either missed his sarcasm or refused to acknowledge it. "Exactly."

"It reminds me of HAL from *2001: A Space Odyssey*."

"That's ridiculous. If I remember correctly, HAL was not nice."

"You slept through ninety percent of that movie. And you were the one who insisted we rent it."

"I was in my all-things-space stage." She sniffed. "It disappointed."

But what David remembered was not disappointment, but that there had been a bunch of them in somebody's basement rec room gamely watching the vintage sixties movie Kayla had rented.

Somehow she'd ended up crammed next to him on a crowded couch. And partway through—after gobbling down buttered popcorn and licking the extra butter off her fingers—he realized she had gone to sleep and her head was lolling against his shoulder, and the cutest little pool of drool was making a warm puddle on his shirt.

And that he hadn't embarrassed her by mentioning it when she woke up.

"How much did you pay for this contraption?" he asked gruffly, moving over to inspect it.

"Fifteen hundred dollars," she said happily. "That's a steal. New ones, of commercial grade, start at ten grand. This size of machine is eighteen thousand dollars."

He realized, uncomfortably—and yet still grateful to have his focus shifting—that Kayla was way more invested in the idea of owning the ice cream parlor than she had originally let on.

"Presumably," he said carefully, "More-moo already has one."

"They don't," she crowed triumphantly. "They buy their ice cream from Rolling Hills Dairy, the same as you can buy for yourself at the grocery store. There is nothing special about that. Why go out for ice cream when you can have the same thing at home for a fraction of the price?"

"Exactly. Why?"

"That's how I plan to be different. Homemade ice cream, in exotic flavors that people have never had before."

She frowned at his silence, glanced back at him. "And, of course, I'll offer the old standbys for *boring* people. Chocolate. Vanilla. Strawberry. But still homemade."

"So what flavor is this that you're experimenting with?" he asked, curious despite himself.

"Dandelion!"

"And that's better than rose petal?" he asked doubtfully.

She nodded enthusiastically.

"Have you done any kind of market research at all?"

"Don't take the fun out of it," she warned him.

"Look, fun is playing volleyball on the beach, or riding a motorcycle flat out, or skinny-dipping under a full moon."

Something darkened in her eyes when he said that, and he wished he hadn't because a strange, heated tension leaped in the air between them.

"Fun is fun, and business is business," he said sternly.

And he was here on business. To return a sweater. But ever since he had walked in the door and felt almost swamped with a sensation of homecoming, his mission had felt blurry.

"That's not what you said in the article for *Lakeside Life*," she told him stubbornly. "You said *if a man does what he loves he will never work a day in his life*."

What did it mean that she had read that so closely? Nothing, he told himself.

"I'd play with the name," she said, ignoring his stern note altogether. "That's part of the reason I like it better than rose petal, well, that and the fact it would be cheaper to produce. I'd call this flavor Dandy Lion."

His look must have been blank, because she spelled it out for him. "D-A-N-D-Y L-I-O-N."

"Oh."

"Cute, huh?"

"Not to be a wet blanket but in my experience, *cute* is rarely a moneymaker. Look, Kayla, if ever there was a time to worry, this would be it. I don't think people are going to line up to eat dandelion ice cream, no matter how you spell it."

"Oh, what do you know?" she said, and her chin had a stubborn tilt to it. "They drink dandelion wine."

"They do? I can't imagine why."

"Well, maybe not the people you hang out with."

"I haven't seen any of the good wineries with dandelion wine," he said, keeping his tone calm, trying to reason with her. "And you can bet they do their homework. In fact, Blaze Enterprises is invested in Painted Pony Wineries and—"

But she turned her back to him, and turned on the machine and it drowned out his advice. He was pretty sure it was deliberate. She freed one arm to open a lid on the top of the stainless-steel machine, then tried to heft the huge bowl up high enough to pour the contents in a spout at the top.

At her grunt of exertion, he stepped up behind her and took the bowl. He gazed down into the bright yellow contents.

"Hell, Kayla, it looks like pee," he said over the loudness of the machine.

Her face scrunched up in the cutest expression of disapproval. "It doesn't! It looks bright and lemony."

"Which, if you think about it, is what—"

She held up her hand, not wanting to hear it. He shrugged. "Whatever. In here?"

She nodded and he dumped the contents of the bowl in the machine through an opening she would have had to stand on a chair to reach.

Unlocked doors. Precarious balancing on chairs. And no phone to call anyone if she found herself in an emergency. Plus, spending fifteen hundred dollars on an idea that seemed hare-brained, and that should still be in the research stages, not the investing-in stages.

Why did he feel so protective of her? Why did he feel like she needed him? She had made it this far without his help, after all.

Though good choices were obviously not her forte.

It occurred to David that he felt helpless to do anything for his mother. And he hated that out-of-control feeling.

Not that Kayla would appreciate his trying to control her. But if he could help her a little bit—find her dog, pour her recipe for her so she didn't risk life and limb climbing on one of her rickety chairs with this huge bowl, save her from throwing away any more money on ice-cream-themed machinery—those could only be good things.

Right?

The machine gobbled up the contents of the bowl with a huge sucking sound. David had to stand on his tiptoes to look inside. The mustard-yellow cream was being vigorously swished and swirled, and the machine was growling like a vintage motorcycle that he owned.

"How long?" he called over the deafening rumble.

"It's going to come out here!" She showed him a wide stainless-steel spigot and handle. "It will be six to twelve minutes, depending on how hard I want the ice cream. We'll try a sample after six."

He peered back in the hole where he had dumped the cream. "Is this thing supposed to close?"

"I'm not sure all the parts were there. I need to look up the manual online. It didn't come with the manual. I saved over sixteen thousand dollars—I can live with that."

The stickler in him felt like now might be a really good time to point out to her that she hadn't actually *saved* sixteen thousand dollars. She had *spent* fifteen hundred dollars.

He had a feeling she wouldn't appreciate the half-empty perspective.

That was one of the glaring differences between them. That and the fact he would have looked up the manual *before* pouring several gallons of pricey cream into the vat.

"You can turn up the beater speed here," she said proudly, and touched a button.

The growl turned into a banshee wail and then the yellow mixture was vomited out of the top of the machine through the same opening he had put it in. It came out in an explosive gush.

He yanked back his head from the opening just in time to avoid having his eyes taken out. A fountain of yellow slush sprayed out with the velocity of Old Faithful erupting. It hit the ceiling and rained down on them and every other surface in the kitchen.

He scrambled for the off switch on the ice cream maker and hit it hard.

The room was cast into silence.

Kayla stood there wide-eyed, covered from head to toe in yellow splotches. One dripped down from the roof and landed on David's cheek.

She began to giggle. He was enchanted by her laughter, and it made him realize there was something somber in her and that she had not been like that before. Not just somber. And not quite hard.

Serious and studious, but not so...well, worried, weighed down by life. As if she had built a wall around herself to protect herself from life.

Suddenly, her laughter felt like a wave that was lifting him and carrying him away from his own troubles. He found himself laughing with her. It felt so good to stand there in the middle of her kitchen and see the hilarity in the situation, to let go of all the dark worry that had plagued him since he arrived home.

Then the laughter died between them.

And then she stepped up to him, and ran her finger across his cheek. She held the yellow smudge up for his inspection, and then, still smiling, she touched it to his lips.

The substance on her finger was already surprisingly chilled, and not quite liquid anymore, but like a frothy, cold mousse.

He hesitated, and then touched his tongue to the yellow glob. In an act of startling intimacy, he licked the substance off the tip of her offered finger.

Was it possible he had wanted to taste her finger ever since she had licked the butter off it all those years ago?

No. That was not even remotely possible.

Still, he was aware that the mess all around him had evaporated. It didn't matter that he was covered in pee-colored mousse, or that it dripped from the ceiling, and spotted the walls and the countertops. It didn't matter that it was splashed all across Kayla's apron and clinging in clumps to her hair.

The flavor on his tongue made him feel as if he was about to die of sheer delight.

Or was the delight because his tongue had touched her finger?

"Well?" she demanded.

"I can't believe I'm about to say this," he confessed, "but Kayla, I think you may be onto something. Don't call it Dandelion. Or Dandy Lion. Call it Ambrosia."

Her smile put the very sun to shame.

So he didn't bother to tell her that her finger was probably a very important ingredient in the ambrosia he had just experienced.

CHAPTER TWELVE

HIS LIPS WERE still way too close to her finger! Kayla wondered whatever had possessed her to touch his cheek, to hold her finger out to him, to invite his tongue to touch her. Something shivered along her spine—an electric awareness of him that was like nothing she had ever felt before.

She could feel her smile dissolving, her pleasure at his approval giving way to something else altogether.

She wasn't an innocent young girl anymore, but the power of her hunger astounded her. She *wanted* him.

It felt like a kind of crime to want someone who had hurt her husband so badly. But had he really? Or had Kevin hurt himself over and over again, and then blamed the whole world in general and David in particular?

She shivered at the thought, and then thankfully, any kind of decision—to lean toward him, to touch his lips with her lips instead of her finger—was taken from her.

He, too, sensed the sudden sizzle of chemistry between them, but he had the good sense to back abruptly away from it.

He turned from her quickly, grabbed a dishcloth from the sink and began to clean up the mess.

That was David. All the time she had known him he had always stepped up to the plate, done what needed to be done.

Especially after the danger of having her finger nibbled, Kayla knew she needed to send him on his way, even if he hadn't received any of the promised ice cream—unless you counted that one taste.

"According to what I read in *Lakeside Life*," Kayla said, "you have better things to do than help me with my messes."

"Don't believe everything you read."

He got a chair and climbed up on it and began to tackle the mess on her ceiling. She saw his shirt lifted and she saw the hard line of his naked tummy.

That hunger unfolded in her, even more powerful than before.

"You should go home." It was self-protection and it was desperately needed!

"I'll just give you a hand with this first."

Kayla wanted to refuse and found that she couldn't. It had been so long since she had had help with anything. Someone to share a burden with was as least as seductive as the sight of his naked skin. For so long she had carried every burden, large and small, all by herself.

An hour later her kitchen had been restored to order. Every surface shone. David had even ferreted out yellow cream in the toaster and wiped it from the inside of the light fixture.

But if the kitchen shone, they were a mess!

"I hope that isn't a Slugs and Snails shirt," Kayla said, but now that she was looking, she could see the distinctive small snail over the left breast.

"Of course it is," he said, glancing down at the yellow blotches that she was fairly certain had already set on his very expensive shirt and shorts. "My company was their start-up investor. I always use the products of the companies we invest in."

A reminder that the man standing here, in her kitchen, covered in yellow stains, was the CEO of a very prestigious company!

He misread her distressed expression. "I'm sure the stains will come out."

"You don't know the first thing about dandelions, do you?" she said, sadly. "When you do your laundry, that stain is not an easy fix."

"I don't do my own laundry," he said, a little sheepishly.

It was a further reminder of who she was sharing her kitchen with. "Well, you could tell whoever does it to try lemon juice."

"Is that why you smell like lemons?" he asked. "Because this is not your first experiment with dandelions?"

He had noticed her scent. Somehow it was headier than dandelion wine.

So when he said what he said next, she should have resisted with all her might. But she didn't have a single bit of might left in her.

"I was on my way down to the lake to swim. Why don't we just go jump in? Like the old days?"

A small smile was playing across the sensuous line of the mouth she had been foolish enough to touch.

She knew exactly what he was talking about. The last day of school, every year, all the kids in Blossom Valley went and jumped in the lake, fully clothed.

And suddenly he did not seem like the CEO of one of Canada's most successful companies. David seemed like what she needed most in the world and had tried, pathetically perhaps, to find in a dog.

He seemed like a friend, and nothing in the

world could have kept her from going and revisiting the most carefree time of her life by jumping in the lake with him!

"Hang on," she said, "I'll grab my lemon juice."

They didn't go to the public beach, but snuck down a much closer, but little-known lake access, between two very posh houses.

He stood patiently while she doused the stains on both their clothes with lemon juice. She set down the empty bottle and then rubbed the lemon into the stains. His skin beneath the fabric struck her as velvet over steel.

She heard his sharp intake of breath and looked up. He was watching her, his lips twitching with amusement but his eyes dark with something else.

Kayla gulped, let go of his shirt and backed away from him, spinning.

"Race you," she cried over her shoulder, kicking off her flip-flops and already running. With a shout he came up behind her, and they hit the cold water hard. He cut the water in a perfect dive, and she followed. The day was already so hot that the cold water felt exquisite and cooling.

The water had been her second home since she had moved here. Beaches and this lake were the backdrop to everything good about growing up in a resort town.

It seemed the water washed away the bad parts of their shared past, and gave them back the happy-go-lucky days of their youth. They gave themselves over to play, splashing and racing, dunking each other, engaging in an impromptu game of tag, which he won handily, of course. He tormented her by letting her think she could catch him, and then in one or two powerful strokes he was out of her reach.

Kayla had known, when she had seen David run the other night, that he had lost none of his athleticism. But the water had always been his element.

His absolute strength and grace in it were awe-inspiring.

That and the fact his wet shirt had molded to the perfect lines of his chest. His hair was flattened and shiny with water, and the beads ran down the perfect plane of his face.

But the light in his eyes was warmer than the sun. That awareness of him that she had been feeling all morning—that had been pushed to the breaking point when she had scrubbed at his lemony shirt—was kept from igniting only by the coldness of the water.

Finally, gasping from exertion and laughter, they rolled over and floated side by side, completely effortless on their backs, looking up at a cloudless sky, the silence compatible between them. Even the awareness that had sizzled seemed to have morphed into something else, like the rain after the electrical storm, calm and cooling.

Finally, she broke the silence.

"I know you didn't lie about him," she said quietly. "David, I'm sorry I called you a liar."

It felt so good that he said nothing at all, rolled his head slightly to look at her then rolled it back and contemplated the blueness of the sky.

The cold of the water finally forced them out. On the shore, she inspected his dripping clothes. The dandelion stains were unfazed by her lemon treatment.

"That will have to be your paint shirt," she said, just as if he was a normal person who actually painted his own home when it needed it.

"Good idea," he said, going along with her. Then, "For two relatively intelligent people, one of us could have remembered towels."

"Watch who you're calling relatively intelligent," Kayla said, and shook her wet hair at him.

"This is a private beach," a voice called.

They looked up to see a woman glaring at them from her deck.

In their youth, they would have challenged her. They would have told her there was no such thing as a private beach. That the entire lake and everything surrounding it to the high water mark—which would take them up to about where her lawn furniture was artfully displayed—belonged to the public. In their youth, they might have eaten their sandwiches on her manicured lawn.

But David just gave the sour-faced woman a good-natured wave, took Kayla's hand, scooped up the empty lemon juice bottle and walked her back out between the houses.

They began the walk home, dripping puddles as they went. Somehow, David didn't let go of her hand. They laughed when her flip-flops made slurping sounds with every step.

She tried to remember the last time she had felt so invigorated, so alive, so free. Oh, yeah. It had been just the other night, lying beside him in the cool grass, looking at the stars.

A siren gave a single wail behind them and then shut off.

They both whirled.

"Oh, no," Kayla said. "It's the same guy."

"She called the police because we were on her beach?" David said incredulously.

Kayla could feel the laughter bubbling within her. "You and I have become a regular two-person crime wave," she said. "Who would have thought that?"

The policeman got out of his car and looked at them. And then he reached back inside.

Kayla squealed.

"Bastigal!"

She raced forward and the dog wriggled out of the policeman's arms and into her own. Her face was being covered with kisses and she realized she was crying and laughing at the same time.

But even in her joy it occurred to her that her dog had been returned to her only when she had learned the lesson: Bastigal was no kind of replacement for human company, for a real friend.

"Did your daughter find him?" David asked. Kayla glanced at him. He was watching her with a smile tickling the edges of that damnably sexy mouth.

"Yeah."

"I guess she's going to be getting that new bike," David said.

"She'll have to find another way to get her new bike."

"What? Why?"

"I told her she can't take the reward. You do good things for people because it's right, not because there's something in it for you. To me, teaching her that is more important than a new bike. Though at the moment, she hates me for it."

"I'm going to buy an ice cream parlor," Kayla said, the tears sliding even faster down her face.

"Maybe you're going to buy an ice cream parlor," David growled in an undertone.

Kayla ignored him. "Tell your daughter she gets free ice cream for life."

The policeman lifted a shoulder, clearly trying to decide if that was still accepting a reward. Finally, he said, with a faint smile, "Sure. Whatever. Hey, by the way, you were called in for trespassing."

"Really?" She shouldn't be delighted, but what had happened to her life? It had surprises in it!

"As soon as I heard *two fully clothed people swimming,* I somehow knew it was you," he said wryly. "I told the complainant she only owns to the high water line."

And then all of them were laughing and the dog was licking her face and Kayla wondered if she had ever had a more perfect morning.

The policeman left and they continued on their way, Bastigal content in her arms.

David reached over and scratched his ears. "He's so ugly he's cute," he said.

"I prefer to think that he's so cute, he's ugly," she retorted. "I think that nice policeman should let his daughter have the reward."

"Do you?"

"Don't you?"

"I don't know. That kind of stand reminded me of what my dad was like," David said quietly.

"I never met your dad," Kayla said.

"No. I think he died a year or two before your family moved here. Completely unexpected. He seemed in every way like a big, strong guy. He had a heart attack. It was instant. He was sitting there having his supper, joking around, and he got a surprised look on his face and keeled over."

"Oh, David."

"No sympathy, remember?" he said. "But keep that in mind. Bad genetics."

He said it lightly, but there was something in his eyes that was not light at all. As if she had been considering him as partner material, that should dissuade her.

How could she address that without making it seem as if she *were* looking at him as partner material?

She didn't have to address it because he went on, his voice quiet, "In the last little while, I've actually felt grateful that he didn't live to see my mom like this."

She wanted to say *Oh, David,* again, but didn't. She was so aware that he was giving something of himself to her, sharing a deeply private side that she suspected few people, if any, had ever seen.

"My dad," he went on, "would have been just like that policeman. He knew right from wrong and he taught me that, and he didn't care if I was happy about it or not. My happiness was secondary to my being a good person."

"Mine, too," she said, "now that I think about it."

"It's nice to see you looking so happy, Kayla," David said quietly, as if they had spoken Kevin's name out loud, as if he knew how desperate she had often felt in her marriage.

She felt as if the tears were going to start again, so she bit the side of her cheek and buried her face in her dog's fur and said nothing.

"It's your turn," he said quietly, as if it were an order. And then, as if she might have dismissed it the first time, he said it again, even more firmly. "Kayla, it's your turn for happiness."

CHAPTER THIRTEEN

Her turn for happiness?

"I feel guilty when I'm happy," Kayla blurted out.

David nodded. "I remember feeling that way after my dad died. How dare the world hold laughter again?"

She nodded. That was how she felt exactly, but it was layered with even deeper confusion because her feelings about her husband's death were not all black and white.

"But then I remembered something my dad said to me," David said thoughtfully. "My dad said you could never be guilty and happy at the same time. Or afraid and happy at the same time. That's why he was such a stickler for doing the right thing. That's what he saw as the stepping stones to building true happiness. And that's what he would have wanted me to do. To choose happiness. And that's what I want you to do, too."

She stared at David. He could have said a million things, and yet the thing he had said was so right.

Despite herself, she shared something else. "David?"

"Hmm?"

"I'm scared of happiness. Remember you said wishes are for children? I'm afraid that the things you wish for just set you up for disappointment. And heartbreak."

They had arrived in front of her house, and he glanced at his and then, as if it were the most natural thing in the world, went and sat in his wet clothes on her front step. He patted the place beside him.

"It was awful, wasn't it?" he asked.

And she was going to say "what?" as if she didn't know what he was talking about, but she did know, and she could not bear to bring dishonesty between them.

She had known this time was coming when they would have to address the history between them.

And she had expected that exploration would be like there was an unexploded mine buried somewhere in the unexplored ground between them.

"Yes," she whispered. "Being married to

Kevin was awful in so many ways. I mean, there were good things, too, don't get me wrong."

"Tell me," he said.

And she knew he didn't mean the good things. She ordered herself not to, but she could not disobey the command in his voice.

And so she found herself telling him. Slowly at first, like water that was seeping out a hole in a dam, the steady, small flow making the hole larger until the water was shooting through it with force, faster and faster.

She told him about the late nights waiting for Kevin, not knowing where he was, about the terrible houses they had lived in and the bills not paid. She talked about working as a waitress and a cleaning lady, about babysitting children and raking leaves, trying to hold it all together long after she should have let it fall apart.

And the more she worked at holding it together the more Kevin seemed to sabotage everything she had done, lose interest in her, treat her shabbily, at first in the privacy of their own home, and then in front of other people.

"Sometimes," she said, finally, "I feel relieved that he died."

It should have been her biggest secret. But it wasn't. There was one left, still.

She waited for him to react with horror to

this revelation that she had never admitted out loud to anyone.

Instead, they sat silently on the front steps with the sun pouring down hot on their heads, drying their clothes so that the lemon stains and wrinkles would probably never come out. Her dog snoozing in her arms, Kayla was aware she did not feel judged at all.

There. They were out. Her shameful and most closely guarded secrets. It *was* like a mine exploding, but instead of feeling destructive, it felt like a relief.

Before it exploded she waited. And wondered. And every step was guarded. And every breath was held.

Suddenly it felt as if she could breathe.

And suddenly it felt as if she were free to walk across the field that was her memory without being caught in an explosion.

Instead of rejecting her, David put his arm around her shoulder and pulled her into the solidness of his body.

And Kayla, in that moment of shared strength and sunshine, realized it had not been so much Kevin she had withheld forgiveness from.

In fact, she had forgiven Kevin again and again and again.

Except when he had died, taking with him any chance that they would find their way, that the love she still had for him would somehow see them through, would fix things—then she had felt angry and beyond forgiveness.

Betrayed by his carelessness in a way she could no longer fix. But now she could see most of her anger was at her own powerlessness.

She realized that more so than with Kevin, it was herself she had never forgiven. She had never forgiven herself for her own bad choices, for making everything worse instead of better.

But there, with David's arm around her shoulder, she felt strong and warm, and for the first time in very, very long, optimistic.

And not in a superficial way. Not about starting an ice cream business or saving a house from ruin. She felt changed in a way that went to her soul.

"Why did you marry him?" David asked, his voice hoarse with caring, knowing instinctively somehow there was one last thing she needed to tell.

She shuddered. The last secret. The thing no one had ever known. Not her parents. Or Kevin's. Not her best girlfriend.

"I was pregnant."

"Shoot," he said softly.

"You would have been proud of him," she

said. "He wanted us to get married. He wanted to do the honorable thing."

But wasn't this also what she had to forgive herself for? That she had accepted his attempt at honor instead of love? That she had allowed it all to go ahead, when there had been a million signs that maybe it would have been better to let it go, even if there was a baby, maybe especially if there was a baby?

"I miscarried the baby a month after we were married. But I still thought I could save Kevin," she whispered. "After that summer, when he changed so much, I thought I could save him."

This was met with silence.

"Love conquers all," she said with a trace of self-derision. "We'd only been together that way once. After that little girl drowned, he was in so much pain. I was comforting him. One thing led to another."

There. Of all of it. That was the thing she had never forgiven herself for.

David's hand found hers, and he squeezed, but then he didn't let go.

"You knew," she whispered. "You knew it was going to be a disaster. You knew Kevin was a runaway train that nothing could stop. You told me not to marry him."

"After that little girl died, it was as if I started seeing Kevin for who he really was," he said, his voice ragged with regret. "He was in pain after it happened. But it wasn't about *her*. It was about how it was affecting *him*. He begged me not to tell the investigators that he hadn't been paying attention that day.

"But I had to do what I had to do. And I could never see him the same after that. I didn't see 'carefree' anymore. I saw 'careless.' I didn't see 'fun-loving.' I saw 'irresponsible.' I didn't see 'charming.' I saw 'self-centered.'

"And still." His voice cracked. "If he would have once expressed remorse for that day, I would have loved him all over again."

His voice firmed and became resolute. "But he didn't. It was always all about him. It gave birth to this cynicism in me that has never been altered. That people will always act in their own self-interest. Myself included. I'm sorry, Kayla. I'm sorry to talk about your husband that way."

But despite the things they both had said, they sat there bathed in more than sunlight.

They sat there bathed in truth and the special bond of a burden shared. They had shared the burden of loving someone who was grievously flawed and all the choices that entailed.

For Kayla, hopeful and romantic, this had meant moving closer. For David, pragmatic and guarded, moving away.

She had judged David's choice, and even hated him for it, but now she wondered if it hadn't been the right one after all. He had saved himself.

And she had lost herself. She had become something she had never been before: cynical and hard and a survivor.

But had she really?

Because sitting here with the warmth of the sun and the warmth of his shoulder being equally comforting, she realized she had never really stopped being that softhearted person who rescued impossible men, and old houses and orphaned dogs.

She had just tried to hide all that was soft about her, because it felt as if it left her open to hurt.

But now she felt soft all over again. She felt soft to her soul and the hard armor around her heart had fallen away, leaving it exposed.

And acknowledging she was those things—someone who believed, still, in the power of love—did not feel like a weakness.

It felt like a homecoming.

Kayla felt as close to David as she had ever felt to another human being. Close and connected.

She tilted her head and looked at him. Really looked. He turned and looked back at her. She saw the most amazing thing in his eyes.

Wonder.

As if he knew he had seen her at her rawest and most real, and *still* liked what he saw.

In David's eyes she saw a truth that stole her breath away. If she were standing with her back against the wall, with the enemy coming at her with knives in their teeth, he would stand beside her.

If they were on a ship that was going down in a stormy sea, he would make sure she was safe before he got off.

If the building were burning and filled with smoke, he would be the one finding her hand and leading her out into the cool, clean air.

He was the one who could lead her to life.

Her newly softened heart was so filled with gratitude that she leaned toward him. She did not know how else to express the magnitude of what she was feeling, what she was awakening to, what she knew of herself that she had not known ten minutes ago.

Kayla found the courage to do what she had wanted to do since the moment she had first laid eyes on him again, after the bee had stung her.

If she'd been dying, she wanted to taste him,

to feel the soft firmness of his lips tangling with her own.

Why would she not feel the same way about living?

He read her intent. And instead of backing away, he moved his hand to the small of her back and brought her in to himself. He tilted his head down so that it was easy for her to reach his lips.

And then they touched.

She touched the soft openness of her lips to the hard line of his. Only his lips were not hard.

Not at all.

The texture was velvety and plump, like a peach, warmed by the sun and ready to be picked.

At first the kiss was gentle, a welcome. But it quickly deepened to reflect the hunger between them, a long-ago fire that still had embers glowing.

Kayla's sense of being alive intensified thrillingly. Her blood felt as if it were on fire. It was *more* than she remembered from that night long ago, because they were both *more*.

More mature, more aware, more experienced. And it felt as if they both brought everything that they were to that kiss, left nothing behind, gave it all. Heart and soul and blood and bone. Hurts and triumphs and all of life.

Her dog woke in her arms, getting squished between them.

Bastigal growled, and then barked and then snapped at David's hand, missing by a hair.

They drew apart. Kayla laughed nervously. "I'm sorry. He's never done that before."

But did David look faintly relieved as he reeled back from her and ran a hand through his sun-dried dark hair?

He was a man who liked a plan. How would he react to the spontaneous passion that had just erupted between them?

It was an earthquake, and he could feel something shifting between them, or the shift in her heart. He let go of Kayla's hand and stood up abruptly. "I should go home and change."

At first she thought he was rejecting her after all. But she couldn't have been more wrong.

"But then I'll come back," he said softly, watching her steadily, letting her know he had seen her and he was not afraid and not scared off by what he had seen, or by what had just leaped up between them, igniting both their worlds.

"You will?"

David nodded. "I need to fix that chair in your kitchen. When I was standing on it, reaching the ceiling, it wobbled pretty badly. I don't want you to get hurt the next time you stand on it to pour something down HAL's throat."

But with her newly opened heart, she saw it wasn't about the chair, really. Maybe it wasn't about her or that kiss, as much as she hoped, either. She saw the look he cast toward his own house.

Something in her said to let him go—but it was the old part, that part of her that somehow had stopped believing that good things could happen and that it was okay to be happy.

The newer part felt stronger. Kisses aside, Kayla could see David *wanted* to have an excuse not to spend time in his mother's house.

He did not have a home to go to, at least not the one next door. She realized he was looking for reasons not go back to the house he had grown up in, not the way it was now.

And whether he knew it or not, or could acknowledge it or not, something about what had just passed between them had let him know she would stand by him.

That she had his back.

Just as she had become so aware that he would stand by her, no matter what.

Kayla had seen the pain and desperation in him this morning. She had nearly wept when he had spoken about how the way his mother was now was threatening to wipe out everything that had happened before.

And she saw the truth. This morning she had been a different person than the one she was now. When had she become that person? The one who would turn away from someone in need to protect herself?

That was what the hardness inside her had done. That was what the bitterness of her marriage had done. That was what being so unforgiving had done.

But those were things that had happened to her. Only she could decide if they could change who she really was.

Really, did anything change the essence of who a person was?

Once, a long time ago, she and David and some other kids had hiked in to Cambridge Falls, not far from town.

But when they had gotten there, someone had left garbage along the edges of the jade-green pool at the bottom of the falls.

She had been incensed, but David had simply picked up the trash and stowed it in his backpack.

"It's temporary," he'd said, seeing her face. "It can't change this." He gestured at the beauty of the fall cascading into the greenness of the glade.

"Even if I didn't pick it up," he'd insisted softly, "five years from now, or twenty, or a hundred, the garbage would be gone, and this would remain."

This would remain. The essence. Water hammering down over moss-covered rocks created a cooling mist and prisms of light, falling into a pool that was the deepest shade of green she had ever seen. Like emeralds.

Like her eyes, David had said.

The essence: what was at the heart of each thing in the universe.

And Kayla felt the garbage had kept her from seeing hers. Now, just as then, David had seen past the garbage, to who she really was.

And had allowed her to glimpse it again, too.

Kayla could feel something fresh and hopeful unfolding in herself. And it made her want to be a better person, even if that meant taking risks.

Surely she could trust herself to be the friend David needed just as he had been the friend she needed this morning?

Or could they ever be just friends after what had just transpired between them?

She drew in a steadying breath at the thought. She remembered his mother in her pink winter boots and her gaping nightgown, and him sleeping on the lawn.

She guessed he was sleeping out there, not just because he didn't like it inside the house, but in case his mother got out again.

He was a warrior protecting his camp, and somehow Kayla had fallen inside that ring of protection.

The tenderness she felt for this strong, strong man who was having his every strength tried nearly overwhelmed her.

Kayla drew in a deep breath. If she could help him get through that, she was going to, even if it meant putting herself in danger.

And being around him did make the very air feel as if it were charged with danger. She was just way too aware of him right now: the rain-fresh scent of the lake clinging to him, his wet shirt and shorts molding the fine cut of his muscles.

And then there was the way his lips had felt on her finger. And then on the tenderness of her lips.

In fact, the place where his lips had tasted her and touched her and claimed her felt, still, tingling, faintly singed as if she had been branded by the electricity of a storm.

"I'd appreciate it if you could fix that chair," she said. "You're right. I would have stood on it to put the cream in HAL."

He nodded, knowing.

"And while you fix the chair, I'll see if I can rescue any of the cream from that machine. We might have homemade dandelion ice cream yet today."

She was pleased that her voice sounded calm and steady, a complete lie given the hard beating of her heart as she recognized a new start, a second chance, a return to herself.

A homecoming.

He shot her a look. "Stay away from HAL," he warned.

"I'm going to rescue my ice cream from the jaws of HAL," she muttered, and heard his snort of reluctant laughter.

"Okay, but don't do it until I get there."

She should have protested at his controlling behavior. Instead, knowing it might be a weakness, she savored someone caring for her.

And she savored caring for someone right back.

"Aye-aye, David," she said, and gave him a mock salute. His grin was sudden, warm, spontaneous, completely without guards; it was the cherry on top of the sundae of what they'd just shared.

"I prefer the French pronunciation," he said, "Duh-veed."

It was an old, old joke between them, a left-over from their high school days, a reminder of the people they both had been, and perhaps, could be again.

CHAPTER FOURTEEN

"AYE-AYE, DUH-VEED," she said, and her laughter felt rich and warm and real as she watched him cross the lawn between their two houses. Then she turned and went around her walkway to her back door, Bastigal tucked close to her heart. She was aware of the dog's heart beating. But even more aware of the beating of her own.

Life.

She was aware she was alive, and glad of it.

A little while later, feeling joyous with her dog back in his little basket watching her, Kayla tried to decide what to wear and what to do with her hair.

Momentarily, guilt niggled at her. What was she doing?

But she brushed the guilt aside and decided right then and there that she had had enough guilt to last her a lifetime. David had said guilt and happiness could not coexist. He had said fear and happiness could not coexist.

When was the last time she had just taken the moments life gave her as a gift? In the past days, lying out under the stars, getting sprayed with yellow globs, swimming fully clothed in the chilly and refreshing waters of the lake she had felt something she had not felt for so long.

Happy.

And then when she had given in to the temptation to taste his lips?

Alive.

And if it was some kind of sin to *want* that feeling, to chase it, even though it was connected to him, well, then she was going to be a sinner.

She had tried for sainthood for the first twenty-some-odd years of life. She was going to try playing for the other side.

And so, she looked at her wardrobe with a critical eye, and she passed over the knee-length golfing shorts and the button-down blouse.

She put on, instead, shorty-shorts and a tailored plaid top that she left one button more than normal undone on.

She scooped up her hair into a loose bun, letting the tendrils fall out and curl around her face. She dusted her eyes with makeup that made them look like they were the color of emeralds, and she dabbed lip gloss onto her lips and admired how puffy and shiny they looked.

She looked at herself in the mirror. She felt attractive and womanly for the first time in how long?

"What the heck are you doing?" she whispered.

Given the hunger David Blaze made her feel, and the happiness, what the heck *was* she doing?

It was obvious. She was playing with fire. And she was startled by how much she liked it, especially when she let him into her house a half hour later and saw the deep male appreciation darken the brown of his eyes to near black.

And then he turned his attention, swiftly, to her rickety chair, and to the heap of tools he had unearthed at his mother's house and brought with him.

For a moment she felt an old wound resurfacing: his turning his attention so deliberately away from her made her feel the same way she had felt after he had kissed her all those years ago, and then turned away.

Suddenly, she wondered about that. Had he turned away then because he felt too little? Or because he had felt too much?

She reminded herself that she had invited him here for him, not for her.

And for now she was going to free herself from all that; she was just going to enjoy the moment. She would navigate the other stuff when it surfaced.

And hope that it didn't blow everything around it to smithereens!

"There," he said, a half hour later, righting the chair, resting his hand on the back of it and looking supremely satisfied with himself when it did not wobble. "Done."

"That's great, David. Hey, do you think you could mow my lawn? I've let it get too deep. I can't even push the mower through it."

He shot her a look like he was going to protest. She deliberately busied herself rescuing the remains of the Dandy Lion ice cream, then snuck a look at him.

As she suspected, David looked nothing but relieved that she had given him another excuse not to go home.

Two days later, on her back deck, Kayla snuck another look at the man in her yard. Terrible as it was to admit—like a weakness, really—it was nice to have a man around. Of course, it didn't hurt that it was a man like David.

They had fallen into a routine of sorts. He

came over in the morning, and she made coffee and toast.

He sat out on her deck with his laptop and used her internet, and then, as if it were a fair trade, did some chores around the house. Her screen door didn't squeak anymore—he'd replaced and reinforced the latch; the kitchen faucet didn't drip.

Yesterday, when the hardware store had delivered planks to fix her back deck, she had protested.

"David, no. I feel as if I'm taking advantage of you and all your manly skills."

He had lifted an eyebrow at her to let her know that he had manly skills she had not begun to test yet. The awareness between them was electric. But despite long, lingering gazes, and hands and shoulders and hips "accidentally" touching, they had not kissed again.

But then his gaze had slid to his own house.

She saw how her initial assessment of the situation had been bang on: he needed to be busy right now.

And his initial assessment of her situation had also been correct: her house was a project that was too big for her to undertake.

"I am so grateful for your help," she admitted.

He smiled and Kayla appreciated the slow

unfolding of the new relationship between them. Even if she would have given in to the temptation, Bastigal had an intuitive sense of when the hum of electricity was growing too intense between them, and would become quite aggressive toward David.

His message was clear: *I am the man of this house.* But in a way it was a blessing that he was chaperoning them.

She had made the mistake of intimacy too quickly once before and the results had been disastrous.

If there was something here to be explored, she wanted to do it slowly, an unfolding of herself and of him.

Now she watched him out on her lawn. David was doing her lawn in sections, mostly because her lawn mower—which he had dubbed HAL Two—had, like the name suggested, a mind of its own.

It would roar to life, work for five or ten minutes and then sputter to a halt. From the first day, she had liked watching David fiddle with her cranky lawn mower.

Every time it broke down he would do the manly things required with such ease: checking the oil, turning it over and cleaning out underneath it. As she looked on he would run his finger along the blade and frown, but then apparently decide it was okay and flip it back up again.

Moments later the air would be filled with the sound of the mower once more. She had always liked that sound and the smell of fresh-mown grass.

Kayla had told herself to keep busy. She could look up the manual for her batch freezer on the internet after all! But there was no reason she could not do that from her perch on the deck.

So she ended up, day after day, taking the computer out on the deck, liking the feeling of being close to him, of covertly watching him work.

Seeing David—willingly working, liking to help out—was such a poignant counterpoint to the life that she had had and the choices she had made.

After watching David struggle through her jungle of a lawn until he was wiping the sweat from his brow, Kayla took pity on him and went in and made lemonade. She had it done by the time the lawn mower shut off, and she called him up from the yard.

He eyed her offering with pretended suspicion.

"This looks suspiciously like pee, too. Is it the Dandelion ice cream reincarnated?"

"No, but what a great idea! Fresh squeezed lemonade at More-moo."

"You need to let me do some homework before you go any further on the More-moo thing."

She went still. Oh, it felt so good to have someone offering to do things for her! But it was a weakness to like it so much, a challenge to her vow to be totally independent.

"Duh-veed," she said, her tone teasing, "I can do my own homework."

He lifted an eyebrow and put down his lemonade in one manly gulp. He handed her the empty glass. "I have people who do nothing else all day long. You should let them have a look at it."

To refuse would be churlish, pure stupid pride. "I'd have to pay," she decided.

"At least that would be a better investment than the batch freezer."

"The ice cream eruption was just a minor glitch," she said. "I can fix it. I've been on the internet looking at that model. The snap-down lid is missing, that's all."

"It's kind of putting the cart before the horse, getting that contraption before you know about the ice cream parlor."

"It was a good deal!"

He rolled his eyes but took the glass from

her. He casually wiped the sweat off his brow. She refilled the glass and he took a long, appreciative swig.

There was something about the scene that was so domestic and so normal that she wanted to just stay here, in this sunny moment, forever.

His phone buzzed and he took it out of his pocket, frowned, read a message and put it back. "Could I tap into your internet for a few minutes? A video is coming through that I'd like to look at on my laptop instead of my phone."

"Of course."

He went and retrieved his laptop from where it was now stored on her kitchen counter. He sat outside on one of her deck chairs. He looked uncharacteristically lost.

Kayla refilled his lemonade one more time. "I hope you don't get a splinter," she said when he thanked her and settled more deeply into the chair.

He looked like he hadn't even heard her.

"Because, Duh-veed, it would be very embarrassing for you if I had to pull a sliver out of your derriere."

"That would be awful," he agreed, but absently.

Suddenly, she was worried about him. He seemed oddly out of it since he had taken that phone call. Now he was scowling at his computer screen.

"Hey," she said softly.

When he looked up he could not hide the stricken look on his face.

"David? What's wrong?"

"Nothing."

"That's a bald-faced lie," she said.

"You've got to quit calling me a liar," he said, but even that was a lie, because while the words were light, his tone sounded as if his heart was breaking.

She had never known a stronger man than him. Not ever. And so it was devastating to watch him turn his computer to her so she could see what he was looking at.

The strongest man she knew put his head in his hands, and she thought he was going to weep.

CHAPTER FIFTEEN

KAYLA TURNED HER ATTENTION to the screen to give David a moment to compose himself. It took her a minute to figure out what she was looking at. And then she knew. It was some kind of retirement home. Unbelievably posh, and yet…

"Oh, David," she whispered.

"I have to put her name on a list. If they have an opening," he said, his voice a croak, "I have to decide right away. I need to go meet with the director and look at the facility in person this afternoon. I'll come back in the morning."

"I'm going with you," she said.

She could not leave him alone with the torment she saw in his face.

He looked at her as if he was going to protest. But then he didn't.

"Thank you," he said quietly.

"I'll go pack an overnight bag. And make arrangements for Bastigal to go to the kennel."

And it wasn't until she was in her room packing that bag that Kayla considered the implications of it. She sank down on the bed.

Life seemed, suddenly, to have been wrested from her grasp, to have all these totally unexpected twists and turns in it.

But there was something about making this decision to go with David that felt as if she had been lost in a forest and suddenly saw the way out.

She *needed* to be there for him. His need and his pain were so intense, and she needed to be there, to absorb some of that, to ease his burden.

Kayla realized there was the potential for pain here, tangling herself deeper in his world. And yet, she had to do it.

The word *love* whispered through her mind, but she chased it away. Now was not the time to study this complication.

Wasn't it enough to know that something amazing was happening, and that it was happening to both of them?

She didn't have to—or want to—put a label on it. She just wanted to sink into the sensation that they weren't, either of them, as alone as they had been just a short time ago.

And she wanted to sink into the feeling of gratitude, that all the events of her life, even her difficult marriage—or maybe especially that—had prepared her for this, made her exactly the person she needed to be to rise to this challenge and more: embrace it.

David was so grateful that Kayla was there with him. It took his mind off what he was about to do. As they drove to Toronto she was the most pleasant of diversions—the way the wind caught in her hair with the top down, how childish she was in her wonder about the car, her lemony scent—what kind of ice cream stain was she trying to get rid of now?—tickling his nostrils.

He wanted to take her for lunch at a place he favored downtown, which was coincidentally close to the "retirement" home, but she took one look at his face and knew he was not up to even the rudiments of ordering a meal.

Instead she had him stop by a food truck, got out and ordered for both of them, and they sat in his car and ate.

"I'll try not to spill, Duh-veed," she said, but quickly saw he was not even up to teasing. She put out her hand and he took it, and it seemed after that he would never let go.

He left the car—she insisted he put the roof up, otherwise he was so distracted he might have left it down—and they walked to Graystone Manor. David knew from the video that it was a converted sandstone house that had belonged to a lumber baron at the turn of the century. It had a specialized wing for dementia and Alzheimer's patients.

The director, Mark Smithson, met them at the door. He was kind and soft-spoken, but nonetheless it reminded David of consulting with a funeral director over his father's ceremony many years ago.

It was a beautiful facility. The rooms were like good hotel suites, the colors were warm and muted, the quality of the furniture and art was exquisite.

As Mr. Smithson talked about their programs for patients with all forms of dementia—people first, illness second, life maps and memory boxes, gardening and crafts—David knew he had come to the right place. He wondered if he should have made this decision long ago.

Still, it was with great sadness that he made the deposit and filled out the forms for his mother.

"We could have a vacancy very quickly," Mr. Smithson warned him, kindly. "You will only have forty-eight hours to make up your mind."

A vacancy. David realized his mother could come here when someone else died. He could not trust himself to speak.

Again he was aware of his hand in Kayla's, and that that alone was giving him the strength to do the unthinkable and unspeakable.

When they left, she remained silent. She did not try to reassure him, or comment on the visit.

Fifteen minutes later, Kayla led him past the uniformed doorman into the lobby of his building. David felt as if he were the Alzheimer's patient, dazed and disoriented.

His condo was Yorkton—arguably Toronto's most affluent neighborhood—at its finest. His company had bought an aging hotel and completely gutted and refurbished it into condos. The lobby, with its Swarovski crystal chandelier, artfully distressed leather furniture and authentic Turkish rugs, could easily compete with the best five-star hotels in the world.

Each condo took up an entire floor of the building; their size was part of the reason they had commanded the highest prices ever paid in Yorkton for real estate.

The elevator, using the latest technology, was programmed to accept his fingerprint. He touched the panel and it began to glide upward to his penthouse.

"But what about company?" Kayla asked, her voice hushed as if she was in a church.

"I can give them a code."

"Oh." She seemed subdued. As the elevator doors whispered open, Kayla looked like a deer frozen in headlights. Her eyes went very wide and David saw his living space through her perspective.

"This is like a movie set," Kayla said.

"Feel free to look around," he invited.

Kayla glanced at him and then moved into his space, her mouth a little round O of astonishment and awe.

The space the elevator opened onto was large and open. The original plank flooring had been restored to distressed glory, stained dark, and it ran throughout.

Low-backed and sleek, two ten-foot white leather sofas, centered on a hand-knotted carpet from Tajikistan, faced each other over a custom-made coffee table, the glass top engineered around a base of a gnarled chunk of California Redwood.

Floor-to-ceiling windows—the window coverings could darken the room by remote control if needed—showed the skyline of Toronto, lights beginning to wink on as dusk fell.

Outside the windows was a generous deck with invisible glass rails. There was a good-sized pool—for a private pool in a condo, anyway—the infinity edge making it seem like the water cascaded off into the city lights. The pool lights on sensors were just beginning to come on, turning the water into a huge turquoise jewel.

The kitchen, open to the living room but separated from it by an island with a massive gray-veined granite countertop, was as sleek and modern as his living room furniture.

"Copper?" she said of the double ovens mounted into the cabinetry. "I've never even heard of that."

"Everybody has stainless," he said.

"Not me," she shot back. "Where's your fridge?"

He moved by her and showed her how the fridge and dishwasher were blended into the cabinetry, artfully hidden behind panels.

"I don't think a fridge like this should be hidden, necessarily," she decided after a moment.

She stared at the built-in espresso maker—also copper—then turned to inspect the copper-topped, eight-burner gas range. She tentatively pushed a button and the range fan silently appeared out of the granite.

"Wow," she murmured. "HAL Three."

He smiled despite himself, glad for the distraction, taking pleasure in her awe of his space. And yet as she looked around in amazement it occurred to him that in the short time he had been in Blossom Valley, her house, with all its unpacked boxes and its old yellow kitchen, felt more like home than this.

This was a space made for entertaining, personally, occasionally. Mostly professionally. The space was designed to impress and it did just that.

She looked at the wine cooler—copper—a dual-zone with French doors.

"How many bottles does that hold?"

"Forty-eight."

"Do you want a drink?" she asked.

He shook his head, "I think that is the last thing I need right now."

She looked so relieved that that was not how he dealt with stress, and he got another hint of what it must have been like with Kevin.

He reminded himself that it was her turn to be happy.

She moved out of the kitchen. When he had designed the condo he had loved it; that by necessity, the windows were only on one wall.

That meant all the rest of the walls, soaring to fifteen feet in height, could be used to display art. Systems of invisible wires, not unlike clotheslines except tauter, displayed dozens of canvasses that he could switch out at any time for others that he kept in a museum-quality storage facility.

"I don't know anything about art," she finally said, "But I stand in amazement. You don't have to understand it. You can *feel* it."

It pleased him that she got it so completely. For a moment a future shimmered before him, the two of them on that couch, sipping wine and...

He made himself stop.

"If you're into a quiet evening in, I'll order us a great dinner," he offered. It occurred to him that Kayla was the only woman he had ever said that to, where he didn't have an agenda.

She crossed over to him and put her hand on his arm. "Right now," she told him sternly, "you do not need to look after me. You need to look after you. What do you need to do for you?"

"I need to swim," he said, nodding toward the pool. "I need to swim and swim and swim. I hope you'll come with me. There's a hot tub, too."

"I didn't bring a suit."

"I keep a supply of them for visitors in the guest suite."

"Ah." She said this a little sadly, as if she was figuring out she did not belong in his world.

And yet the truth for him? His apartment had never felt as much like home as it did with her looking through his kitchen.

"Will you swim with me?"

For a moment she looked as though she was going to bolt for the door. But then she drew in a deep breath and nodded solemnly.

"I'll show you the guest suite," he said. "Suits are in the top drawer, left hand side, in the closet."

Kayla heard the door of the guest suite whisper shut behind her. She looked around at the opulence, almost shocked by it.

There were in here, as elsewhere, floor-to-ceiling windows. The same beautiful, dark, aged hardwood ran throughout.

An antique four-poster bed, centered on a deep area carpet and beautifully made up with modern-patterned bedding that contrasted the age of the bed, looked incredibly inviting.

It was a walk-in closet with built-in shelves and drawers and hangers. She went to the top drawer on the left and found a huge selection of bathing suits, all brand-new and all sizes, from children's to men's.

Somehow it was a relief that he didn't just entertain women here!

Tempted as she was to snoop through the other drawers, Kayla chose several suits that might fit her and went into the bathroom.

Again, she was nearly shocked by the opulence. There was a fireplace! In the guest bathroom! A beautiful painting hung above it. There were dove-gray marble floor tiles, honed, instead of polished. Despite the fireplace, the focal point of the room was definitely an egg-shaped, stand-alone soaker tub. Two lush and obviously brand-new white robes hung from hooks. Towels, plush and plump, also pure white, were rolled into a basket by the tub.

Kayla tried on three of the suits, feeling just a bit like Goldilocks. The first one was too skimpy, the next one was too frumpy and the third one was just right.

Darkness had fallen almost completely when, wrapped in one of the housecoats, she slid open the door of her suite that went directly onto the patio.

The view was breathtaking and the pool was gorgeous, lights inside it turning the water to winking turquoise.

Aware David was already in the water watching her, she slipped off the housecoat and slid into the water.

She made her way over to him and sat on an underwater bench beside him.

"Thank you for coming today," he said hoarsely, "I don't think I could have made it through without you." And then wryly, "Kayla to the rescue."

"She'll be safe there," Kayla told him. "And as happy as can be expected. I liked the memory box idea. What will you put in it, I wonder?"

David was silent for a long time. When he spoke his voice was so low that Kayla had to strain to hear it.

"I'll put the pinecone Christmas ornament I made in the second grade in it," he said. "And the corsage my dad gave her for their fifteenth anniversary that she dried and always kept by the bed. I'll put the dog's worn old collar that she kept long after he died and that still sits on the mantel. I'll put in my graduation diploma. I'll put her favorite recipe book in there, and a picture of her sister and the old sepia photo of the farm she grew up on in Saskatchewan. I'll put in the ugly dish that she made in ceramics that we all laughed about, and the earrings I gave her for her birthday when I was ten, and that she wore even though they looked like Ukrainian Easter eggs.

"A whole life," he said, his voice breaking. "How can I put her whole life in a box? How do I put in Canada Day fireworks, and the look on her face as she looked upward? How do I put in the memory of her fingers on my back as she smoothed cream on a sunburn? How do I put in waking up to the smell of bacon and eggs? How do I put her laughter when the snowman toppled over? How do I —" But he didn't finish.

He was crying.

She had never seen a man cry. It seemed to her it was the strongest thing she had ever seen a man do.

It seemed to her she had never seen a man so capable of deep love and the sorrow that it brought.

She slowly moved her hand and caught one of his tears and lifted the saltiness to her lips with gentle reverence and tasted it.

He caught her hand and he kissed it and then he moved away from Kayla, sliced cleanly through the water and began to swim.

And after a moment she dove into the water and she swam beside him, silently, matching him stroke for stroke, swimming through the silent beauty of a dark city night, swimming through the memories that swirled around them, swimming through the pain.

She would not have chosen to be anywhere else at that moment but beside him, swimming through life in all its grief and all its glory.

CHAPTER SIXTEEN

WHEN IT SEEMED like they had swum for hours, David hoisted himself out of the pool and then helped her out.

His body was extraordinary, beaded with water, the city lights and the reflections from the pool casting it in bronze. His swimming trunks clung to the perfect muscle of his legs.

"Can I interest you in that dinner now? I'm hungry."

"Liar," she said, softly. "You're just saying that because you think I should eat something."

He smiled tiredly.

"Why don't you go to bed?" she said. "I'll look after myself tonight."

"Are you sure?"

She nodded. After he had gone, she sat on his big couch and watched the lights outside.

After a while, she went into that opulent guest suite, put on her pajamas and got into the giant bed. She could not sleep and got up, took the housecoat from where she had dropped it on the floor, wrapped it around herself and wandered restlessly around the gorgeous apartment. She was drawn to the art.

Even in the darkness, it held light. She moved slowly from one amazing piece to the next. It was almost too much beauty to take in.

Then Kayla froze when she heard a sound. She moved out of the living room and went down a wide hallway in the direction she thought the sound had come.

It was a different wing than the guest room was in, and she realized it was his wing, where his private bedroom suite was.

She found herself standing outside his bedroom door.

It was slightly ajar and she could hear the steadiness of his breathing behind it. She was going to move away when the sound came again, a stifled sound of pain, like a wounded animal.

She gave David's bedroom door a faint shove with her fingertips and it whispered open. Like the rest of the apartment, the bedroom could have been from a movie set, or a hotel suite that rented for thousands upon thousands of dollars a night.

He had not bothered to close the drapes, and the floor-to-ceiling windows looked out over the dazzling lights of the city. The pool lights were reflecting in the room, making it seem like an underwater dream.

It was a deeply masculine room, done in many shades of gray, but saved from being too cold or too modern by an exquisite large abstract painting—an explosion of warm colors—that hung above a bed that was enormous.

The bed, despite its kingly proportions, struck Kayla as being faintly sad, like two people who didn't like each other very much could sleep here and never know of the other's presence.

The sound came again, a muted sound of torment, and she slipped deeper into the room and tiptoed over to the bed.

He was fast asleep, his lashes long and thick and casting faint shadows against his cheeks. A faint bristle was rising along the line of his jaw. The covers were thrown back and David was bare-chested.

The masculine lines of his chest put the beauty of the canvas above his head to shame!

His legs, clad in Slugs and Snails pajama bottoms in a different shade than the other ones she had seen, were tangled in the sheets. It was obvious, from the messiness of the bed coverings that his sleep was restless and troubled.

In his sleep, David's brow furrowed, and he made that sound again, tormented.

Tentatively, she put her hand on his forehead and was satisfied when, under her touch, he was soothed and the line of distress left his brow.

It felt like a stolen moment, a guilty pleasure, to study him like this without his knowledge, to drink in the now oh so familiar planes of his ruggedly handsome face. It was with the utmost of reluctance that Kayla turned away.

"I don't want you to go."

At first she thought he was talking in his sleep, talking about the decision he had made for his mother, that he did not want her to have to leave her home of forty years and go to Graystone Manor.

But when she turned back, prepared to soothe again, David was awake, if groggy. He drank her in, then propped himself up on one elbow and drank her in some more.

It was probably only the lateness of the hour, the magical light reflected from the pool outside his bedroom, but it seemed to her that the look in his eyes might be identical to the one she had just looked at him with.

He scooted over in the bed and tapped the empty place beside him with the palm of his hand. Her mouth went dry. She felt as if she were standing on the edge of a cliff, deciding whether to jump or to back away.

To jump held the danger—and the thrill—of the unknown. To back away did not really feel like an option at all.

Feeling powerless she slipped in beside him, and felt not the danger of a leap into the unknown at all. She lay on her back, studying the ornate plaster work on his ceiling, feeling the exquisite touch of linen warmed through by his skin.

She felt that softness within her swell like a bud in early spring about to burst.

He covered her with the sheet. "What have you got on underneath that housecoat?" he asked gruffly.

"My pajamas."

"Are they sexy?"

"No."

He growled something that she was pretty sure was *thank God*.

She nestled into him, cherishing this moment, feeling as if she were in a dream that she didn't want to wake up from.

"David," she said after a long time, trusting the sense of intimacy between them, "I need to know something."

"Anything."

"Why did you stop talking to me that night after you kissed me?" she whispered, needing, finally, to address the last of the unfinished business between them.

He closed his eyes again. She heard a ragged regret in the quietness of his deep voice.

"Kevin told me he'd asked you to the prom. To me, it was an honor thing between friends. You don't take your best friend's girl. He had spoken for you. I took the step back."

She was silent as she contemplated this. Kevin had not asked her to the prom until after David had kissed her. She had only said yes because it was evident that David regretted the kiss, and had no intention of taking his relationship with her anywhere. Maybe she had even hoped it would make him jealous.

Certainly, picking out the prom dress, she had been thinking of David as much as Kevin. That she would be gorgeous, and he would be sorry that he had let her get away.

But David had not reacted to her at all that night. He'd seemed engrossed in Emily Carson, who had been wearing a pure black strapless gown that made her seem sophisticated and worldly and that had made Kayla feel like a small-town girl and a hick that a guy like David would never look at.

This knowledge—that Kevin had betrayed her, betrayed both his friends, manipulated and lied to have his own way—did not have any taste of bitterness to it.

She had already forgiven him.

And she had already forgiven herself.

She saw no point in telling David. Wouldn't the knowledge just cause him more pain when he was dealing with enough?

Plus, it was as if knowing that final truth about Kevin set her totally free.

To love another. Or perhaps to return to the love her heart had first recognized.

"David?"

"Hmm?"

"You loved him, didn't you?"

There was a long silence, and then he said, "Yeah. He was not just my friend. He was my brother."

A floodgate that had been closed opened between them.

The water of forgiveness flowed out of it and washed over both of them.

"Tell me something wonderful that you remember about your brother," she said softly. "Remind me of the Kevin he once was."

And so he did. And then she did. And then he did. And by the time the morning light had softened the room, they were exhausted.

"I always thought," David said, "if I stopped being angry with him that all that would remain would be a pool of sadness so deep I would drown in it."

"And?" she whispered.

"It doesn't feel like that at all. It feels as if the love remains, strong and true, even after all we went through. I wish I could tell him."

"I think you just did," she said softly. "I think you just did. He gave us more than he took, didn't he? Even his flaws helped shape both of us into the people we are today.

"Do you think," Kayla went on, "that is what love does? Performs this kind of alchemy, where it turns lead into gold?"

No answer. She turned and gazed at him. David was sleeping, not restlessly now, his arm curled around her, his nose buried in her hair.

"I love you," she whispered.

Maybe he was not sleeping after all because she felt a sudden tension ripple through him and she braced herself for his rejection.

But it did not come. Instead, he sighed and relaxed, and the arm that was curled around her touched her hair, and then pulled her in yet closer to his heart.

Any thought about going back to her own room evaporated. She could not resist lying beside him, just for a moment, just to drink in his scent and the feel of his skin, to feel the heartbeat of the man she had come to love so completely.

His essence.

But somehow, her eyes closed and she fell asleep beside him.

David awoke feeling groggy, as if he had a hangover, when he knew he had not had a drop to drink. That was the power of grief.

He stretched and then froze, opened one eye and then the other cautiously.

Kayla was in his bed, her small frame wrapped in the plushness of the housecoat, her face squished against his skin, her beautiful honey-colored hair scattered across his naked chest. If he was not mistaken, there was the tiniest little pool of drool on his chest.

The feeling of grogginess left him, as did the feeling of being hungover.

It seemed to David, in a life that had everything—glamour and adventure and success beyond his wildest dreams—that he had never had a moment sweeter than this one.

It occurred to him he loved her.

And that maybe he always had, from that first kiss.

And so he savored her head on his chest, and the lemony scent of her. Had she said those words last night?

Had she whispered *I love you* to him?

The moment of sweetness was replaced with sadness. There was a responsibility with loving someone. As she had said last night, loving Kevin had shaped them both. Even his flaws had shaped them. And this was one of the things David had learned.

To love someone was to protect them from harm.

It made David feel like a colossal failure, given the decision he was about to make concerning his mother.

To love someone was to protect them from pain, not to cause it.

He thought of what that meant in terms of what he had been discovering over the long, lazy days of summer, about what he felt for Kayla.

There was no chance—absolutely none—that they would grow to love each other less. No, he knew that.

He knew each tumbling snowman, and each summer night lit with fireworks intensified the love. He knew that old dogs died and new puppies came home, and that these events intensified the love.

And so did making ice cream.

And so did cleaning up messes that dripped

from the ceilings and covered their clothes in yellow splotches.

And lying on the lawn looking up at Orion and listening to her name the stars.

And swimming fully clothed in a cold lake on a hot summer day.

And what did that mean, that the love kept deepening and intensifying? It meant it would hurt Kayla more when that day came.

When the doctor's reassurances about his heart proved incorrect and, just as it had done for his father, that vital organ exploded inside his chest and left him lying on the floor, keeled over, dying in front of her, all the chest compressions in the world not enough.

Or when they were walking through someplace like Graystone, only this time it was her decision to make. About him. About what to do with him.

All the money in the world and all the success could not stop the march of time. All the money in the world could not rip the "E" gene from your body and replace it with something else.

All the money in the world could not prevent the inevitability of causing those you loved pain.

Kayla woke up slowly and he cherished her waking. He cherished her slow blink, and then nodding back off, a stir of her leg, and then her arm, her hand pushing her hair from her face.

And then that hand settling on his chest. And going still. Her eyes popping open wide, taking it all in.

And then her smile.

He would hold that smile in his heart forever. And then she leaned over and kissed him. And for one horribly weak moment, he let himself believe he could have this. That he could really have it all.

And then he yanked himself back from her, sat up, swung his legs off the bed and kept his back to her.

In a voice stripped of emotion, he said, "What are you doing in my bed?"

He could not turn and look, but he could feel the sudden stillness in the air.

"Isn't that exactly what got you in trouble before?" he said into her stricken silence. "Weren't you trying to make someone feel better who was in pain?"

Again, the silence that was worse than words.

He made himself look at her. He made his voice as hard and cold and mean as he could. He said, "I don't need you to rescue me, Kayla. I don't need you at all."

All those times she had seen him so clearly, all those times she had called him a liar. He held his breath hoping, maybe even praying, that she would see the lie he was telling her now.

But she didn't.

Her face went blank with pain. After the intimacies of their conversation last night—of finally reaching that place where the love and forgiveness flowed, instead of the anger—he felt his own treachery deeply.

And then she got up out of his bed, stiffly, and with her head held high, without glancing back, she walked out of his room, shutting the door quietly behind her.

It was only after she was gone that he let himself feel the pain of what he had just done. And he couldn't just let her go. How the hell was she going to get home? Walk? Take a bus?

He went and threw open his bedroom door, folded his arms over his naked chest, watched her heading for his door, her little overnight bag so quickly and haphazardly packed that something pink—the panties he had caught sight of that first day—were caught in the zipper.

When she heard him open his bedroom door, she tucked her head down so that her hair fell in a smooth curtain over her face, and hurried faster toward the elevator.

"I'll have a car sent around for you," he said, his voice still stripped of emotion, cool.

Her head shot up and she looked at him.

"Let me tell you something, David. Kevin never asked me to the prom until *after* we kissed that night."

He schooled his features not to show the distress that made him feel, not to let the thousand *what-ifs* that leaped instantly to his mind show on his face.

With humongous effort, with a kind of negligent carelessness, David lifted one shoulder, as if he didn't care.

Through the tears, she said a word he suspected she had never ever said before.

And she added a very emphatic *you* to the end of it.

And then she was gone.

CHAPTER SEVENTEEN

KAYLA HAD NOT BEEN out of her pajamas in a long time. Weeks? Her eyes were nearly as swollen from crying as they had been from the beesting. She was afraid to look at the calendar. How many days of summer had she let slip away while she nursed this heartbreak?

"Pathetic," she told herself. "You are pathetic."

Bastigal, her stalwart companion, licked her tears and looked worried.

Kayla took another spoonful of the ice cream out of the big tub on the coffee table in front of her.

It was bright yellow. It *did* look like pee. But it tasted surprisingly good, even after consuming nearly a gallon of it, solo.

Bastigal liked it, too, and uncaring about what it said about how pathetic her life had become, she let him share the spoon with her.

She had known the truth all along. The

heartbreak had been completely preventable. David was completely out of her league after all. Look at that car. And the way he dressed. And that apartment. There was a fireplace in his bathroom, for Pete's sake.

David Blaze was straight out of a magazine spread, Kayla reminded herself glumly. He dated actresses, and ran a multimillion-dollar corporation. They *still* had stacks of that magazine all over town. She could not avoid his handsome mug, even when she ventured out ever so reluctantly to get dog food.

It made her mad that she had *hoped*. It made her even madder that David had presented himself as a regular guy who could mow the lawn and fix the door.

Who, even though he owned a zillion-dollar condo, had slept on his back grass to protect his mother.

Ten days after she had left his Yorkton condo, an ambulance had pulled up next door. She had raced to put on her shoes and get over there to see what was wrong with Mrs. Blaze, but as she had opened her front door, David had pulled up.

In a different car. Sleek and black and very, very expensive-looking. A uniformed driver had gotten out and held the back passenger-side door open for him then waited at a kind of respectful distance while David went into the house.

And she had sunk back in the shadows, realizing the ambulance had not come with its sirens on, so it was not an emergency. His mother was being transported to Graystone.

And she realized the difference in their two worlds.

Kayla realized he was this man: in the expensive suit, with the chauffeur holding open the door for him.

And yet, when he had come back out, his mother strapped to the ambulance gurney, the stricken look on his face had nearly made her go to him.

But his words that morning, brutal, had come back to her.

Isn't this exactly what got you in trouble before? Weren't you trying to make someone feel better who was in pain? I don't need you to rescue me, Kayla. I don't need you at all.

And so she had resisted the impulse to watch him from behind the sheer curtain in her living room, to see if he would even glance this way. Instead, she had turned away from the terrible tragedy of the scene unfolding next door, and gone to her couch.

And she had rarely been off it since.

The dog was a safe bet. The best bet. She had

been on the right track when she had sworn devotion to her dog and her house and her business.

Would she buy More-moo? What if David was right? It was just risky business, one more hopeless rescue.

Her doorbell rang, and Kayla started, and the dog leaped off her lap and raced in crazy circles in front of the door.

She couldn't go to the door. She was in her pajamas. She had barely combed her hair since she had come back from Toronto. She had not brushed her teeth today. And possibly not yesterday, either. She had yellow splotches down the front of her pajamas.

Then it occurred to her.

It was him. It was David. His mother was settled in Graystone. He was coming out of that terrible crisis with a new understanding of what mattered. He had come to declare the error of his ways. He had come to get down on bended knee, beg her forgiveness, perhaps ask her hand in marriage.

Her heart thudding crazily as she contemplated a world once again ripe with possibility, Kayla slid off the couch and crept to her living room window, lifted the shade a hair.

It was another bright summer day and the

brightness hurt her eyes. A courier van was pulling away.

So it was a written declaration of error, a written proclamation of undying love.

She went and flung open the door and looked at the parcel that lay there in its plastic envelope. The return address, Blaze Enterprises, seemed to be blinking in neon.

She picked it up and hugged it to herself, waltzed through to the kitchen—which was a disaster of ice cream and HAL experimentation—and went to her cutlery drawer. She found a butter knife and slit open the envelope.

She pulled out a thick binder and frowned. That would be quite a lengthy apology. And declaration of love.

She flipped it over and read: More-moo, A Financial and Business Analysis.

The self-pity evaporated instantly and was replaced with furious anger. Without opening the cover of the binder, Kayla went over to her garbage can, stepped on the lever that opened the lid and tossed the whole thing in.

It landed amongst the empty cream containers.

She stared at it for a moment, and then said a word she was saying for only the second time in her life. She added a most emphatic *you* after it.

And then she went into her bedroom and

took off the stained pajamas, and decided, after looking at the stains, that they would be best beside the Business Analysis binder in the garbage.

She showered, put on her favorite white skirt, a dusting of makeup and her big, white sun hat that only a little while ago had made her feel independent and carefree and faintly Bohemian. She kissed Bastigal goodbye, knowing it would be a struggle to get him back in the basket, and then went and wheeled her bike out of the shed.

She rode downtown.

She felt a love for Blossom Valley swell in her heart as she rode down Main Street. The July sun had gentled into the cooler days of August. The leaves on the trees hinted at changes, and the summer crowds were thinning as people headed back to the city to do their before-school shopping.

She parked her bicycle in the rack outside More-moo, and looked hard at the place. The awning looked tired and the petunias had gotten leggy.

Still, she looked beyond that. It was only cosmetic, after all. Kayla took a deep breath and setting her shoulders, she went and opened the door.

It was a screen door on squeaky hinges, and

a bell croaked a raspy greeting as she entered. Inside it was dark and cool after being in the bright sun.

It smelled good, and the little old lady beaming welcome at her from behind the counter reminded her of the grandmother she had always adored.

It wasn't as crowded as it would have been in the height of summer. She was sure that would be in the report.

But something the report wouldn't have captured was a young family of three sitting at one of the round tables, on the wrought iron, curly-backed chairs with the round seats padded in red-checked vinyl. The baby, in a baby seat, was covered in chocolate ice cream, the whites of his eyes showing like those of a miner coming up from the coal, the mom and dad laughing at him as he yelled for more.

In the booth in the corner, a boy and a girl sat across from each other, their fingertips intertwined in the center of the table. They were so delightfully young—maybe fifteen—and a single shake, in thick glass showing above metal shaker, was between them, with two straws but they were just using one, taking turns.

She recognized Mr. Bastigal, the science teacher, long since retired, nursing a coffee and looking forlornly out the window. He still looked like the spitting image of Albert Einstein. Someone had told her his wife had died last year, and he looked lost. His gaze flickered to her but without recognition. Had she known she was going to bump into him from time to time, she probably would not have named the dog after him.

All of it: the smells and the sounds and the people, the unfolding of life's beautiful, simple vignettes filled her with a feeling.

No business report in the world could give you this: the feeling that something was just right.

Kayla walked up to the counter. The woman smiled at her as if she were a long-lost relative who had found her way, finally, home.

"I'd like to talk to someone about buying your business," she said firmly.

CHAPTER EIGHTEEN

Up until now in his life, David Blaze had been blessedly unaware that it was possible for a human being to feel as bad as he felt.

He barely slept. And he barely ate.

Guilt gnawed at him. And it wasn't guilt for the decision he had made about his mother. That had been a decision absolutely necessary to her health and well-being. It hadn't really been a decision at all, the choices narrowing until there were none left.

Now that his mother was settling at Graystone, he really wondered why he had waited so long. They were set up beautifully for her care. She was safe there. And relatively happy. Plus, she was closer. He could stop in and spend a few minutes with her every day.

Sometimes they went through the memory box, and it brought him great comfort to see her fingers gently stroking the petals of that dried rose corsage, as if the details of what it meant might be lost to her, but the essence was not.

He had put in an old nozzle from a garden hose to remind her of the skating rink, and then an old photo of him and Kevin standing in that rink, looking at the camera. That photo, of them leaning with fake ferociousness on their sticks, seemed to be her favorite thing in the box.

She touched David's younger face in the photo with such tenderness. "This is my son," she said. Some days she remembered his name, and other days she didn't, and she almost never made the connection it was that same son who sat beside her now. And yet by her face, David was reassured that she remembered the most important part about the skating rink, too.

The devotion that had built it.

And the boys who had skated there had known that love built it, even if they had not ever said that. The boys had loved each other, even if they had never said that, either.

And when she touched his face in that long-ago photo, he felt she remembered what was crucial, at the heart of it all, the essence.

The love.

What he felt guilty about was that he had chased Kayla away and made her feel as if it was in any way about her.

He had made her feel her ability to love and to hope were a defect of some sort, and his regret was sharp and intense, a companion that rode with him and tormented him daily.

It was just wrong. He was a man who had built his whole life and his entire career on integrity, and the lie he had said to Kayla ate at him.

He had made it sound as if he didn't care about her. It had been for her own good, but it still didn't sit well with him. He had a sensation of having to set it right.

His assistant, Jane, came in.

"How's your mom today?" she asked, her face crinkled with concern.

He knew she was seeing the changes in him: weight loss, dark circles around his eyes. He had snapped at her more in the last few weeks than he had in all the years they had worked together.

She was putting it down to stress over the decisions he had made about his mother, and he was content to leave it at that. He didn't think he could handle one more woman thinking he needed rescuing.

"What's up?" he asked her, not answering about his mother, who was, in fact, having an off day.

"This just arrived by courier. I know you were waiting for it."

David looked at the sealed envelope she handed him. The return address was from Billings and Morton, an independent laboratory. It could take weeks and even months to get this kind of information. Though he rarely used his power or wealth to circumvent the system, he had this time.

"Thanks," he said, setting the envelope aside.

Jane turned to leave, and then turned back. "Oh, one more thing. Do you remember that ice cream parlor you asked me to do the analysis on?"

He nodded, hoping the sudden tension did not show in his face.

"The one that, in the final analysis, was about the worst investment anyone could ever make?"

He didn't nod this time, only held his breath.

"Somebody bought it," Jane said with a faint derisive giggle. "Can you believe that?"

Actually, he could.

"Just a sec," she said, "I've got the name of the person out on my desk."

"Never mind," David said. "I already know."

And he waited until she had closed the door behind herself before he contemplated the completeness of his failures when it came to Kayla McIntosh Jaffrey.

He thought, to his own detriment, he was always so colossally sure of himself. He always was sure he was doing the right thing.

Look at all those years ago, when he had backed off Kayla for Kevin, thinking it was the honorable thing between friends.

And it had been based on a total lie.

Kevin hadn't asked Kayla to the prom by then. Someone else who had been at the campfire that night must have told him about what had happened between David and Kayla. And Kevin, ever competitive, ever with something to prove, had scooped him on the girl.

To Kevin, it had probably all been a game.

Until Kayla was pregnant.

Still, he knew that he was experiencing a miracle of sorts, that when he thought of Kevin these days, it was never with anger. It was with the quiet tolerance of knowing he had loved someone flawed, and that he had grown from it.

Once he had thought his love for Kevin had only given him the gift of cynicism. Now he saw that it had given him many gifts, but that was the one he could leave behind.

He hoped all that love that was part of his history would show him the right thing to do now. When he opened this envelope, wouldn't he know he had done the right thing by love? David reached for the envelope, turned it over in his hands and yet could not bring himself to open it.

It was time to set everything right that had gone wrong. It was time to end the lies. There was no place in life for deceit.

The next thought came unbidden, *Maybe it was time to let someone else into my world. Maybe there was less chance of making a mistake with a decision when it was not made alone, and when all parties were armed with the facts.*

That thought gave him pause. He *always* made the final decision alone.

Why did it feel like such a relief to even be contemplating a different way?

"Bastigal, stay away from the paint. Oh, for Pete's sake." Kayla got down off the ladder, caught Bastigal and wiped the creamy white paint from where his tail had dipped in the open bucket. She secured the lid on the bucket and headed back up her ladder, paint brush in hand.

From her perch there, she paused and looked around.

Really, if she was going to be painting, she could have started at home. But no, she was excited about More-moo. She had kept it open until the long weekend in September, learning all she could from the outgoing owners, and giving out samples of flavors she was experimenting with. She was excited about the response.

Then she had shut it down completely to freshen up the inside and bring in new equipment before reopening with a brand-new menu and services. She would be reopening in October.

She could almost hear a cynical voice saying, *Who comes to Blossom Valley in October?* That thing happened in her heart that happened every single time David crossed her mind, which was still pathetically often.

The new copies of *Lakeside Life* had replaced the old, but that didn't help as much as she had hoped it would.

Because it seemed the very streets held memories, of their younger selves, yes, but of the time they had just shared, too.

She could not look out her back window without picturing him stretched out on the back lawn at his mother's house. She could not open the screen that did not squeak anymore without thinking of him. Or secure the latch without remembering his dark head bent over it, the tip of his tongue caught between his teeth in concentration. She couldn't get the lawn mower going at all, and that made her think of him, too.

There were streets she avoided altogether, like Peachtree Lane, where they had lain on their backs after chasing the bunny they thought was Bastigal, and she had named the stars on Orion's belt for him.

Even on the hottest day, Kayla would not swim in the lake, because the memory of swimming with him, fully clothed, and the sense of awakening that had come with that, were painful.

When she was not busy painting or chipping fifty-year-old linoleum off the floor of her new business, she tried to stay busy so she wouldn't think so much, fall into the trap of feeling sorry for herself.

Kayla was experimenting with all kinds of flavors of ice cream—rose petal, jalapeño jelly, nasturtium, even dark ale—but for some reason the Dandy Lion flavor seemed to be on hold.

The door jingled, and she realized she had forgotten to lock it, and even a small thing like that made her think of David, and that he would be irritated with her for giving safety such a low priority.

"Sorry," she called from her perch on the ladder, "we're closed."

Bastigal began to growl, that low, throaty sound she had only heard him make on a few occasions before—mostly when she and David were getting too close to each other!

She turned on the ladder, felt the shock of who was there as if she had conjured him by thinking of him so much!

Her fingers felt strangely numb and she nearly dropped her container of paint. In her attempt to keep her hold on it, she lost her balance.

He was beside her in a second, lifted her easily from around the waist and settled her solidly on the floor.

The dog, of course, went crazy as soon as David touched her, and ran a frantic circle around them, barking.

"I got paint on your nice suit. Sorry." She stepped away from him, trying not to stare, trying not to drink in his features like she was parched and he was a long, cold drink of water.

"David," she said, and heard some softness in her voice—the softness she had revealed to him and he had then used to hurt her. Keeping that in mind, she recovered, set down her paint and folded her arms over her chest.

She tried not to feel dismayed that he looked so unwell. Had he been sick? He looked like he had lost fifteen pounds, and there had not been any extra flesh on him to begin with! There were dark circles under his eyes, and his cheeks were whisker shadowed. His hair was a little long in the back, touching his white shirt, curling a little around his ears.

Kayla realized she wouldn't be much to look at at the moment, either. She really regretted the disposable painter's coverall that made her look a little bit like a snowman.

"What are you doing here?" she demanded, so afraid to hope for anything anymore, steeling herself against the crazy flip-flopping of her heart.

"Full price, Kayla? Are you crazy? You could have waited for spring to buy. That's closer to your very small money-making season."

She should have known that's why he would have come! A poor business decision was as irresistible to him as she had once hoped she would be!

She stripped the disappointment from her voice. "How do you know I paid full price? Have you been spying on me?"

He looked a little sheepish.

She had no intention of letting him know that her heart quickened at the very thought he was keeping tabs on her, that he cared even a little bit. She wanted desperately to ask him how his mom was doing, and how he was coping, but his last words reared up in her head.

And he was right. Feeling for people was

always what got her in trouble—trying to fix their pain was her worst flaw.

"You should have offered less if you were taking it at the end of the season. You think people are going to be eating ice cream for Thanksgiving? If, by some miracle, you manage to reopen by then?"

"I'll be open by then," she said stubbornly. "I'm doing two specialty ice creams for Thanksgiving, a pumpkin and a cranberry."

"Appealing," he said sarcastically.

"I don't care what appeals to you," she lied.

He flinched, and she wanted to take it back, but she didn't. She stood there waiting to see why he had come.

He drew in a deep breath, shoved his hands in his pockets and studied his shoes, which looked very expensive.

Bastigal ventured in and sniffed them, backed off growling. He managed to leave a white paint mark on the toe of one.

"Understandable," David said, "that you would not care what appeals to me. I'm afraid I hurt you."

"Nonsense," she said quickly, but her voice had a little squeak in it.

He went on as if she had not denied it. "The last time I saw you, I was a jerk, Kayla."

"Yes, you were."

"You aren't going to make this easy for me, are you?"

"No, I'm not."

"I wanted to hurt you," he said slowly. "I wanted to drive you away."

"I'd say that worked. I had a very nasty bus ride back to Blossom Valley."

"I offered you a driver."

"Big of you. I made the most of my bus ride. I thought of ice cream flavors the whole way," she lied, and then, as if she could convince him it was not a lie, "Hot Banana Pepper, Cinnamon and Pear, French Champagne, Chinese Noodle."

She had not really thought of any of those flavors until just this second. All of a sudden it penetrated the almost panicky sensation that she could not let him know how she really felt, what he had actually said.

I wanted to hurt you.

That was not David.

I wanted to drive you away.

"I couldn't leave it the way it was," he said. "Kayla, I could not leave you with the impression that it was about you. That it was because I didn't care about you. Or need you."

Her heart felt like it stopped in her chest. What was he saying? That he *did* care about her? That he *did* need her?

She took in his ravaged features, and suddenly saw, as if a light had been turned on in a dark room.

She saw so clearly it felt as if she would explode.

David Blaze *loved* her.

CHAPTER NINETEEN

"KAYLA," DAVID SAID, his voice barely a whisper. "My family has a long history of health problems. I wouldn't wish them on anyone."

From her memory bank she pulled a sentence. *No sympathy, remember?* he said. *But keep that in mind. Bad genetics.*

He had said it lightly, but there had been something in his eyes that was not light at all.

It had been that day when they were walking home, dripping from the lake, and the young policeman had reminded him of his father.

And he had told her how his father had died.

"You think you're going to have a heart attack. Like you dad," she said softly. She was aware her voice was trembling as the truth of why he had come here filled her up. To the top. And then to overflowing.

"That might be a mercy compared to the other thing."

"The other thing?"

"It can be genetic," he said softly. "What my mother has. They've isolated a gene. It's called the E gene."

He pulled an envelope from his pocket and handed it to her. She took it, not understanding. She glanced at if briefly and read the return address: Billings and Morton. It meant nothing to her.

"It's from a laboratory. They do independent genetic analysis."

"Oh, boy," she said. "And you're lecturing me on wasting money foolishly? What did this cost?"

"That's not the point!"

"I bet this cost nearly as much as my new flooring," Kayla said.

"You are missing the point. This is very serious business, Kayla," he said tersely. "I was tested. Open it. And then we'll know."

"Know what?"

"Whether," he said softly, "I am worth taking a chance on."

She stared at him, and then she began to laugh. Into his astonished features, she said, "Oh, you stupid, stupid man."

He looked stunned. Well, obviously as the head of one of Canada's most successful companies he had never heard that before.

Then he looked annoyed, and folded his arms over his chest.

Who was really the stupid one, Kayla asked herself? She should have figured this out. She'd known from the moment she saw him sleeping on his mother's back lawn, guarding the door, that this was what he did. He protected those he loved.

And when he could not protect? When it was not in his power?

Then he retreated, to nurse his sense of failure, impotence in the face of what mattered most to him.

She saw in a brand-new light why he had never renewed their friendship after she had married Kevin. Had it ever been about Kevin at all? Or had it been about his own love for her? And how he would hide that, especially when he saw she was unhappy or needed his protection.

The love had been there between them for so long, constrained, and now it was breaking free.

She felt her love for David quicken within her. It felt as if a light had gone on, that was filling her and then expanding beyond her, filling the room and then beyond that, the street.

It felt as if the love within her could, unleashed, reach out and fill up the whole world.

Kayla looked down at the envelope in her hands, and then, without opening it, she ripped it to shreds.

"Hey!"

"No," she said firmly, throwing the pieces of paper up in the air and watching them scatter. "We're going to pretend we opened it. And we're going to pretend it said yes."

"Yes?" he said, flummoxed.

"Yes." She nodded emphatically, and crossed the space that separated them. She reached up and ran her palm over the rough surface of his whisker-bristled cheek.

"We're going to pretend it said yes. And that you went to the doctor and he told you that you had heart disease, too. We're going to pretend you could die any second."

He stared at her, baffled. And annoyed.

And yet she could see the hope in his eyes, too, so she went on, her confidence and her certainty increasing with each word she spoke.

"And while we're at it," Kayla said, "we're going to pretend I went to someone who could tell the future. Who is famous for it and never gets it wrong. A gypsy woman with a head scarf and too much makeup and earrings as big a pie plates looked into her crystal ball—"

"You are not comparing a legitimate medical laboratory like Billings and Morton to a fortune teller!"

"Yes, I am," she continued, unperturbed by the interruption. "The gypsy woman said I was going to get hit by a car and die instantly."

"Stop it," he said.

"No, you stop it."

He looked stunned. Really, being the head of a large company had made David Blaze far too accustomed to being listened to, even when he was wrong.

"Don't you see?" Kayla asked him, suddenly serious. "Don't you get it, David? We are going to live like it said *yes*. We are going to live each and every day as if one of us could be gone. Instantly. Or just disappear without warning from the face of the earth. Or change beyond recognition.

"And that is going to allow us to celebrate this moment. We are going to drink each other in, as if this day, this very second, might be our last together. As if everything could change in a moment.

"And we're going to start like this."

She stood on her tiptoes and she took his lips with her own. For a moment, he held himself stiffly, resisting.

And then with a moan of complete surrender, he kissed her back. He wrapped his hands in her hair and pulled her so close to him that not even air could squeeze in between them, and certainly not her overexcited dog!

Bastigal ran frantic circles around them, yapping hysterically.

"Bastigal," David said, taking his lips from hers for just a second. "Hush up and get used to it."

The dog fell silent. Then he sat down abruptly and stared at them, worried. And then his tail began to thump cautiously, then joyously, on the floor.

If there is anything a dog recognizes, it is the absolute essence of what is going on.

David let go of his last need to control, to protect Kayla from the folly of loving him. He drank in what she was giving him.

She loved him. She loved him completely and deeply and he realized, astounded, that he needed the *way* she loved him.

Kayla's way of looking at the world was opposite to his own.

He was pragmatic. She was whimsical. He was sensible. She was impulsive. He was ruled by his mind. She was ruled by her heart.

Her way was not wrong. And neither was his. But each of them only formed half a picture. They needed each other to come into perfect balance.

And he was aware that maybe he needed her a whole lot more than she needed him. He had walked alone for too long, battered by the ravages of love: his father, Kevin and now, his mother.

She, too, was battered. But she was the one with the courage to say yes to all of it. To the storm, and to the rainbow. To the tears and to the laughter.

It occurred to him that Kayla would show him the very heart of what love meant. And as he took her offered lips, it felt as if he was sealing a deal.

That would give him the life he had always dreamed of, and been afraid to ask for. A life that was so much more than a great condo and a fleet of cars and a successful business.

A life that was full in a different way, and a better way.

A life that was full in the only way that really counted.

And so David began his courtship of the girl he had always loved. And he courted her as if she might be gone from him at any second, or he from her, and as if it was a sacred obligation to cram as much joy and as much life into those seconds as they could.

He soon realized it didn't matter what they were doing, whether they were jumping into the amazing colors of the sugar maple leaves that they had raked in her yard in Blossom Valley, or attending a black-tie art auction in New York.

It didn't matter if they were throwing snowballs at each other after the first snow, or getting ready for the charity Christmas Ball Blaze Enterprises held every year. It didn't matter if they were having a quiet glass of wine in his apartment, watching the New Year's Eve fireworks explode over the city or sitting with his mother, taking pleasure from her enjoyment in the CD Kayla had picked out for her.

It didn't matter if they were having a croissant at a bakery, after he'd convinced her they should go to Paris for springtime, or whether they were supervising the installation of the new ice cream cooler at Dandy Lion's Roaring Good Ice Cream getting ready for the grand reopening.

It didn't matter if he was watching the awe on her face as she saw the Louvre for the very first time, or if they were paddling a canoe across the lake, trying to keep Bastigal from jumping in after the ducks that swam beside them.

It didn't matter if she was asleep with her

head on his shoulder in the airport lounge after their flight had been delayed because of fog, or if he was covered in grease from trying to get that old lawn mower going for one more season. She wouldn't let him buy a new one. She claimed that old lawn mower was going in her memory box someday.

"Everybody else gets a memory box," he teased. "Trust you to get a memory crate."

But the truth was they were going to need a crate to store all these memories in!

As spring began to turn to summer once more, David watched his calendar, and a year to the day that he had seen Kayla riding her bike down the main street of Blossom Valley, a year to the day that she had been stung by the bee, he proposed.

He had the ring put in a special box that he had custom made. The box was yellow and black and shaped like a bumble bee.

For the ring he had chosen a perfect, brilliant white diamond mined in the Canadian arctic. He had consulted on the design of the setting, wanting it to reflect Kayla's personality, simple but complex, light but deep.

On the day that marked the anniversary of their meeting again, while Kayla was busy overseeing things at her astonishingly busy ice cream parlor—people were actually driving from Toronto to sample some of those crazy flavors like jalapeño Havarti, for Pete's sake?—he brought a team into her backyard.

And they transformed it.

White fairy lights were threaded by the thousands through the trees and shrubs. A structure was erected at the center of her yard, a gauzy tent, and inside it was a table set on a carpet that covered the lawn. The table was covered in sparkling white linen, set exquisitely for two.

Every available surface inside that tent was either full of candles or flowers.

A chef was working magic in her kitchen and at her barbecue. A waiter stood by, elegant in tails and white gloves. A string quartet was set up in one corner of the yard to supply music.

David had even managed to get Bastigal into a tux that matched his own, right down to the subtle pink of the bow tie, and pleased with himself for this detail, he had fastened the ring box onto the back of Bastigal's suit, and then locked him in the house.

And that's where things went wrong.

Or right, depending what kind of memories you wanted to put in your memory box.

Because everything had gone perfectly. The dinner was exquisite. The music was beautiful. The summer evening night was soft with warmth and fragrance.

Kayla was gorgeous, sitting across from him, in her white Dandy Lion uniform, laughing and crying, and then laughing again.

Once, he had seen himself as pragmatic, and her as the believer in miracles.

But wasn't he living a miracle? He and Kayla had had a chance to love each other once, and circumstances had taken that chance from them.

Now they had been given what he saw as the rarest and most beautiful of gifts.

"Here's to second chances," David said, lifting his champagne flute to Kayla's.

A second chance that was made better by the fact that both their lives had given them things that had made them stronger and ultimately better, more ready for what an adult love required.

On cue, just as they finished dinner and before dessert, when he could not wait another second with his secret, with a quickly lifted finger from David, the waiter casually went across her back deck and let Bastigal out of the house.

David knew the little dog, having missed her all day, would make a beeline for Kayla and deliver the ring.

Except at the very moment when the dog was hurtling himself across the yard in a paroxysm of excited welcome for Kayla, the chef was flambéing dessert at their table.

At the sudden poof of blue flame, Bastigal stopped. Then he tucked his tail between his legs and with a single startled yip, ran away and, though it seemed impossible, squeezed himself underneath the gate and was gone.

It seemed like a full minute of stunned silence fell between them.

And then David leaped up and took chase, with Kayla hard on his heels, and the chef scowling at their departing backs and his ruined finale.

It seemed it was hours later that they finally caught up with the little dog after doing a backyard and alleyway tour of most of Blossom Valley.

They captured the dog and Kayla admired his little outfit and David retrieved the ring, and she laughed at the little bumble bee box and she laughed right until the moment that David got down on bended knee in front of her.

Then the tears came. She had Bastigal clasped to her chest and tears running down her face, whether from laughing or crying, he wasn't too sure.

And he wasn't too sure it really mattered which it was, either. Because the essence of that moment was startling in its clarity, more multifaceted and brilliant than the ring he was about to give her.

"Will you marry me?"

The look on her face was a look that could make any man find the courage in himself to believe in the future.

She had not said yes, yet, when a spotlight caught them in the harshness of its glare.

"Sheesh," David heard a voice behind him say, "I should have known."

Kayla's laughter was better than a yes. It was the laughter of a woman who wasn't the least bit guilty about her happiness. It was the laughter of a woman who did not have one ounce of fear in her.

Her joy filled her eyes with a light that drenched him, and that drenched the world around him, turning it from black and white to pure gold.

This, then, was what his future held.

EPILOGUE

ONCE, DAVID BLAZE THOUGHT, he had been the most arrogant of men. Had he really believed that he knew the things that intensified love? Had he really been convinced he knew of the things that should be included in a memory box?

Now he was humbled by how little he had known.

The moment Kayla and he had stood on a beach in the Caribbean, she in a sundress and a spaghetti-strapped T-shirt and a hat that reminded him of the day she had bicycled back into his life, he had felt the love between them intensify to what he believed was a breaking point.

But then, when she had whispered *I do,* his love had intensified to such a point that he did not know how a heart so full could not explode. He had been sure it could never get fuller. Or better. Or more intense.

When the doctor had sat him and Kayla down, and smiled slightly and said *congratulations,* that was the moment he realized something in him was expanding to hold a whole new level of intensity.

But it surely had reached its limit now? His heart was fuller than full. It could not expand any more.

But then it did. Any other intensity David had ever experienced had been eclipsed by the ultrasound pictures.

And then that had been eclipsed *again* by that terrifyingly beautiful night when David would have done anything to take the pain from his wife.

And then *that* moment moved into the shadows when he held the baby in his arms, that wrinkly, loud, ugly, hair-sticking-up-every-which-way bundle of life that was his daughter.

And now, Kayla punched the code on the door, simple one-two-three, but more complicated than anyone on the wing could figure out, and they went down the hall to his mother's room.

His mother was sitting in a chair, and when they came in, she looked at them blankly. He was thankful that today, at least, she had her clothes on.

But then she saw the baby, and something soft bloomed in her face.

Not recognition of them, perhaps, and perhaps that was not what was as important as what she recognized, anyway.

She looked eagerly at the bundle he was holding, and held out her arms.

He glanced at Kayla. Was it okay to give their daughter to his mom? Who admittedly was not all there? Could this poor addled soul be trusted with something so fragile as a baby, less than a week old?

But Kayla nodded without the slightest hesitation.

David passed the baby to his mother, ready to rescue her in an instant if something went wrong, but it did not.

He felt himself relax as something went beautifully, wonderfully right.

It occurred to him that this was a moment he would put in his memory box, the way his mother's instinct was still there, and her one hand went naturally to cradle the baby's neck while the other supported her tiny body.

This would surely always be in his memory box, his mother's face when she held her granddaughter. It was as if everything else they had been through was gone, and there was only this moment of shining truth left.

What the memory box held—the only thing of any importance at all—was the love.

An experience so intense that by some miracle it took the limits off a human heart, letting it expand beyond measure to hold it.

"Her name is Polly," he said softly.

"But that's my name," his mother said, bewildered.

"Yes," he said quietly. "Yes, it is."

The two Pollys regarded each other solemnly. And then the baby wrinkled up her face, opened her eyes and blew spit bubbles from her lips. She made a cooing sound and she blinked and she wriggled a little bit, tiny fists finding their way out a pale pink blanket and flailing at the air.

And the light that came on in his mother's face held every Christmas morning, and every fireworks display they had ever seen together, and it held the puppy he had brought home. It held safe the memory of his father, and all that they had been as a family. It held his friendship, his brotherhood, with the boy next door.

The light in his mother's face held joy and tears, and sorrow and laughter.

And Kayla's hand crept into David's and he looked down at her and saw the contented smile on her face.

Of all the gifts she had given him, and those

were many, he was aware of how tenderly she had revealed his dishonesties to him.

And this was the biggest one: once, he had convinced himself that he could not go to her because he was protecting her from his bad genetics.

Now he saw not that he had wanted to protect her, but that he had wanted to protect himself. Because to love greatly meant a man had to open himself to the possibility of great loss.

Unbearable loss, even.

And yet, that same love he feared, when he turned his face to its sunshine, did not burn him, but day by day lifted him up and filled him with a simple faith.

It was a faith that for all the bad, the good still won out, still outweighed the bad ten to one. Or maybe a hundred to one. Or maybe even a million to one.

And in the end, it seemed to David, when everything else was gone, even the memories, you could trust one thing.

The love remained.

In the end, you could trust that the intensity of love, the essence of it, remained and traveled— relentlessly, unstoppably, breathtakingly—toward the future it had helped to shape.

* * * * *

LARGER-PRINT BOOKS!

GET 2 FREE LARGER-PRINT NOVELS PLUS
2 FREE GIFTS!

◆HARLEQUIN®

Romance

From the Heart, For the Heart

Enjoy this sneak preview of
NINE MONTHS TO CHANGE HIS LIFE
by Marion Lennox, the first in our life-affirming
The Logan Twins *duet!*

"It's a biggie."

"What's a biggie?"

Deep breath.

"Learning you're about to be a dad."

She was so aware of his body.

"I've been thinking I'm glad you don't want a termination," he said.

She stilled. He was watching the toast. She was watching the breadth of his back. To all intents and purposes they were a couple talking cozy domestic things—like termination.

"Why?" she managed.

"It's been a shock," he said softly. "All afternoon…all tonight… Heaven knows how you slept but I couldn't. I wouldn't have wished for it, but now it's happened… I do want this child."

There was a lot to think about in that statement. A lot to make her heart falter?

"One part of me's pleased to hear you say that," she admitted at last. "I was never going to terminate, not for a moment, but in a way, I think that's why I came here so early in the pregnancy. I needed to know your reaction. I wanted my choice to be your choice."

"But the other part?"

Say it like it is, she decided. *Just say it.* "Another part of me almost had a heart attack, just this minute," she admitted. "Do you want this child like you want another Logan? And how much do you want it? Enough to sue me for custody? I hadn't even thought about that."

"I would never do that to you. And she's your baby."

"She?"

"I thought tonight…" He looked at her for a long moment, his expression unreadable, but when he spoke, it was all tenderness. "I thought, what if she's a girl, just like her mother?"

What was there in that statement to take her breath away? What was there in that statement to make her forget where she was, to forget everything except those words?

What if she's a girl, just like her mother?

She'd been terrific when she'd found out she was pregnant, she'd decided. She'd surprised herself by how calm she'd been. She'd set about making plans, figuring how she could manage.

She'd decided to tell Ben, rationally and coolly. She'd prided herself on her efficiency, getting a passport, figuring flights, choosing the hotel Ben so rudely rejected.

She'd told him calmly. Everything was going as planned.

But one little statement…

What if she's a girl, just like her mother?

She sat on the bench and stared, and suddenly the cool control she'd kept herself under for the past couple of months snapped.

She couldn't help it. Tears were rolling down her cheeks, and there wasn't a thing she could do about it. She couldn't speak. She just sat there and cried like a baby.

This was a woman who seldom cried. He knew that. What was happening now was shocking her—as well as shocking him.

She needed tissues, but his shoulder was closer. He stepped forward, gathered a sodden Mary into his arms and held her.

He was cradling her like a child, but this was no child. She'd slumped against him, but the slump had turned to something more. Her face was buried in his shoulder, but the rest of her… She was molded to him. Her breasts were pressed to his chest. His face was in her hair.

"I can't…" It was a ragged whisper.

"I have it in hand," he told her, and before she could make any objections, he swung her into his arms and strode with her into his bedroom.

NINE MONTHS TO CHANGE HIS LIFE by Marion Lennox, available June 2014, only from Harlequin Romance—don't miss it!

And look out for the second title in this wonderful duet, THE MAVERICK MILLIONAIRE by Alison Roberts, available July 2014.

HREXP05i